Praise for *Winning the War in Your Mind*

Winning the War in Your Mind is a must-read for those who want to identify patterns of unhealthy thinking and what to do about them. So much about life is won or lost in our thoughts. This incredible book is packed full of research, biblical truths, and insightful paradigm shifts that will help you win the daily battles inside your own head. I plan to give this to every member of my family. It's that good!

—Lysa TerKeurst, #1 *New York Times* bestselling
author; president, Proverbs 31 Ministries

We can't change what we don't see, and we can't bring to Jesus what we won't take the time to understand. This book is filled with insights from a voice in my life I've trusted for a decade. Craig helps us understand how our minds are wired, why we do what we do, and how we can take our next courageous steps forward in our faith.

—Bob Goff, Sweet Maria Goff's husband

If you're like me and have struggled with anxiety or negative thought patterns, this book is for you. Pastor Craig does an incredible job with relaying how we can change our thinking so that God can transform our lives. The best part is that he uses psychology *and* the Word to bring us truths. This book will show you how to envision your new life and stop believing the lies of the enemy.

—Sadie Robertson Huff, author, speaker, founder of Live Original

Believing lies robs us of the life God intends for us. Through the scope of Scripture and science, Craig gives us powerful strategies to defeat the lies, change our thinking, and win with God's truth.

—Dave Ramsey, bestselling author and radio host

Your thinking determines your destiny. Whether you think you can or think you can't, you're right. This book will give you tools to renew your mind through the power of God's Word so you can live a passionate, purpose-filled life and fulfill your destiny.

—Christine Caine, bestselling author; founder, A21 and Propel Women

Practical and profound. There are few people more skilled than Pastor Craig Groeschel at taking a theological truth and unweaving the tendrils of confusion to get to the clear, meaningful application. That is why I am so confident that this book will both challenge and lead readers toward fruitful life change. I believe that this topic is essential to the holiness of every believer, so this book is a must-read.

—**Louie Giglio,** pastor, Passion City Church; founder, Passion
Conferences; author, *Don't Give the Enemy a Seat at Your Table*

Since childhood, I've known that the difference between successful and unsuccessful people is in the way they think. It's a lesson my father taught me, and it has guided me to this day. In his new book, my friend Craig Groeschel brings both science and biblical wisdom to bear on the process of thinking, and shows you how you can change your thinking in order to change your life.

John C. Maxwell, founder, The Maxwell Leadership Enterprise

It's time to step out of old ways of thinking and start heading toward the life you could be living, a life in which your thoughts no longer control you. I've personally needed these lessons from my friend Craig Groeschel, and I'm so glad he's sharing them with you in his new book.

—**Steven Furtick,** pastor, Elevation Church;
New York Times bestselling author

Craig is a bold leader who has committed his life to giving away truth to our generation. He's a worthy guide through this important topic.

—**Jennie Allen,** author, *New York Times* bestselling *Get
Out of Your Head*; founder and visionary, IF:Gathering

Craig has taken his trademark enthusiasm to see people win, coupled it with an understanding of brain science and his ability to communicate God's Word, and put it in this book. As you read these pages, there's a pretty good chance your brain and your heart will do a little dance.

—**Michael Jr.,** comedian, author, thought leader

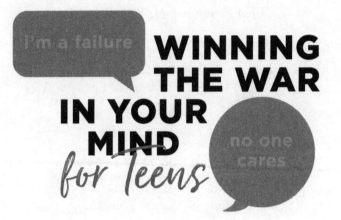

WINNING THE WAR IN YOUR MIND
for Teens

i'm a failure

no one cares

Also by Craig Groeschel

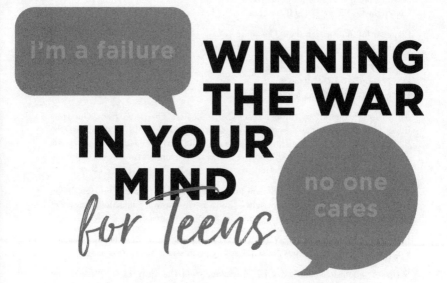

WINNING THE WAR IN YOUR MIND
for Teens

I'm a failure

no one cares

CHANGE YOUR THINKING, CHANGE YOUR LIFE

CRAIG GROESCHEL
WITH JOSH MOSEY

ZONDERVAN®

ZONDERVAN

Winning the War in Your Mind for Teens
Copyright © 2023 by Craig Groeschel

Requests for information should be addressed to:
Zondervan, 3900 Sparks Dr. SE, Grand Rapids, Michigan 49546

ISBN 978-0-310-14544-8 (hardcover)
ISBN 978-0-310-14547-9 (audio)
ISBN 978-0-310-14546-2 (ebook)

Zondervan titles may be purchased in bulk for educational, business, fundraising, or sales promotional use. For information, please email SpecialMarkets@Zondervan.com.

Craig Groeschel is represented by Thomas J. Winters of Winters & King, Inc., Tulsa, Oklahoma.

Cover design: Micah Kandros
Author photo: Life.Church
Interior design: Denise Froehlich

Printed in the United States of America

22 23 24 25 26 LBC 5 4 3 2 1

This book is dedicated to my children.
You do more with your partially developed brains than
a lot of grown folks do with theirs, your dad included.
I love who you are, who you are becoming,
and who God made you to be.

contents

introduction

What Makes the Teenage Brain Unique?

Let's start with a story from my teenage years. Yes, I was a teen once. Yes, I know saying that to teens doesn't earn me any credits because it happened so long ago. We're four sentences in and already getting off topic.

Imagine teenage Craig. It's the 1980s. Malls are all the rage. Every home is covered in dark wood paneling. I'm out riding my bike without parental supervision. Everyone rode their bikes everywhere and parents had no idea where their children were.

The wind is whipping through my hair (because bike helmets weren't a thing back then). I am about to attempt something so cool that the neighborhood will forever remember Craig "the Daredevil" Groeschel. That's right; just like Tom Cruise, I do my own stunts.

I'm flying down the street on my sleek, metallic-blue Schwinn ten-speed with a lightning stripe across my blue seat. (Why a lightning stripe? Because I'm quick, dangerous, and full of raw energy.) I take one foot off the pedal and place it on the crossbar. I slowly rise and place my other foot on the bike seat.

Cool, right? What could go wrong?

My hands are still on the handlebars, so I'm kind of squatting while I fly down the road. I lift my foot off the bike seat, thrusting my leg high toward the sky. If "Lightning Bike Yoga" was a thing, this move would be called the *majestic crane facing a glorious future* or maybe just *the sweet Groeschel*. But squatting while lifting my leg isn't the thing that'll cement my name in the Book of Stuntmen. I want to surf.

I arrange my feet. My left remains on the crossbar behind the handles. My right returns to the bike seat. I look up. Wind is streaming past me.

I take one hand off the handlebar.

So far, so good.

I start to take the other hand off . . .

And I wake up in the hospital.

• • •

Being a teenager is like riding a bike, but the road conditions keep changing, your bike seat isn't the correct height anymore, and bystanders are yelling different directions at you while you pedal along. It's more than a stressful ride, and you're still discovering just how hard it is to be a teen. Even without trying to surf your bike—instead of riding it like a sane person—the road can be dangerous.

Do you know what my parents asked me when I woke up in the hospital?

Of course you do.

"Craig, *what* were you thinking?"

• • •

What were you thinking?

The teenage brain is incredible. According to neuroscientists—aka brain doctors—teen brains have an over-abundance of gray matter (the stuff where information gets stored) and an undersupply of white matter (the stuff that wires different parts of the brain together to help information get where it's needed).

Your brain is at peak efficiency for learning and can tuck away information more efficiently than at almost any other time in your life. That's awesome! At the same time, your brain is super inefficient when it comes to being able to pay attention to something for long periods of time. And skills like self-discipline, task completion, and handling emotions are still being developed while the areas of the brain are connecting to each other.

This isn't a value statement on your worth or capabilities. It's a biological truth that our brains aren't fully wired until sometime in our mid-twenties.

Teen brains have less ability to process negative information than adults and are less likely to learn from their mistakes or misadventures. Remember teenage Craig trying to surf on his bike? Do you think that was the last stupidly risky thing I did? (It wasn't.)

Now, before you start using the "my brain isn't fully developed yet, so I can't help but make dumb choices" excuse with people, know this: Your brain and its development stage right now are a gift from God and you are responsible for using it appropriately. We all may have reasons why some things are more difficult for us than others, but there are never excuses.

The good news is that your brain is also more capable of learning good, helpful behaviors and life-changing habits right now than at any other time due to something called neural plasticity.

What Is Neural Plasticity?

Neural plasticity is the brain's ability to change, which is basically what learning is. The word "plasticity" comes from the Greek word *plastikos*, which has to do with molding something—it was usually clay in ancient Greece—into a certain form. Although we think of plastic as the stuff we recycle (like bottles and packaging), it gets its name from the fact it was molded into a certain shape before it hardened.

Every time you learn something new, your brain flexes and molds new connections between the thing you're learning and stuff you already know. As you might guess, babies have the highest levels of neural plasticity because they are learning everything for the first time—but teens still have wildly impressive brain plasticity. It isn't until around age twenty-five that a person's super-ability to learn tapers off to average (or at least not as impressive) levels.

What does that mean for you? It means your brain is perfectly poised to learn. Just remember that with great power comes great responsibility (thanks, Spider-Man!).

• • •

We're going to get into all kinds of interesting terms and explore some basics of how the brain works, but this book isn't a science book. I'm writing it because there's a war going on and your brain is the battlefield. What you think right now will shape who you are and who you will become.

That's not an exaggeration. Our lives follow the direction of our thoughts. The better you can understand that now, the better equipped you'll be to change the trajectory of your life. Throughout this book, we'll unpack both Scripture and what we've learned from scientific research. Check this out:

In Philippians 4:8–9, the apostle Paul writes, "Finally, brothers and sisters, whatever is true, whatever is noble, whatever is right, whatever is pure, whatever is lovely, whatever is admirable—if anything is excellent or praiseworthy—think about such things. Whatever you have learned or received or heard from me, or seen in me—put it into practice. And the God of peace will be with you."

In these three sentences, Paul moves from

- ► thought ("think about such things") to
- ► action ("put it into practice") to
- ► experience ("the God of peace will be with you").

Paul tells us that our thoughts shape our lives.

In recent years, an entire discipline of modern psychology has developed called cognitive behavioral therapy (CBT). This breakthrough teaching reveals that many problems—from eating disorders to relational challenges, addictions, and even some forms of depression and anxiety—are rooted in faulty and negative patterns of thinking.[1] In CBT therapy, treating those problems begins with changing that thinking.

I don't know about you, but when the Bible and modern psychology say the same thing, I want to know more.

What Is Cognitive Behavioral Therapy?

 Cognitive Behavioral Therapy, or CBT, was developed in the 1950s and 1960s by psychiatrist Dr. Aaron T. Beck. Dr. Beck wanted to understand the relationship between our thoughts and how we act. For instance, if you think, *I hate school and no one likes me*, you are probably not going to put in extra effort to do well in school or connect with other students. Group projects would be an even bigger nightmare than they already are!

But if you can think something true and helpful, your behavior can change and lead you to better thoughts. Like saying, *School may not be fun right now, but doing well makes it possible to do what's important to me later in life. I feel unliked right now, but that feeling will pass and I'll find the right group of friends later on.*

Dr. Beck's research was later backed up by brain science. Later in this book, we'll learn some helpful ways we can hack our brains so they better deal with life while also looking at how we can grow a deeper faith.

Material based on *Your Amazing Teen Brain: CBT and Neuroscience Skills to Stress Less, Balance Emotions, and Strengthen Your Growing Mind* (Instant Help/New Harbinger Publications, 2022) by Elisa Nebolsine, LCSW, p. 3–4.

How Can You Make Your Brain Work for You?

In ten years, we will each look in the mirror, and someone will stare back. By that time, your brain is going to be fully wired. You'll have full access to all the hidden features that come with the right connections. Those connections—and that person in the mirror—will be shaped by the thoughts of today.

The life we have is a reflection of what we think.

That's out there, right? What we think will determine who we become tomorrow. And we probably don't even realize it's happening! We don't think about the power of our thoughts, which only makes them that much more powerful. But God made us this way. What science is showing us today is what God told us through Solomon almost three thousand years ago: "For as he thinks in his heart, so is he" (Proverbs 23:7 NKJV).

So if both the Bible and modern science teach us that our lives are moving in the direction of our strongest thoughts, then we need to make time for introspection and ask ourselves, "Do I like the direction my thoughts are taking me?"

If your answer is no, either in general or in any specific area of your life, then maybe it's time to change your thinking. Decide to change your mind so God can change your life.

If you are sick and tired of having toxic thoughts invade your mind, of being held hostage by those inner voices, I want to encourage you to keep reading and stay open. Whether or not you consider yourself a Christian, I promise there are truths in these pages that will work if you put in some effort to apply them.

As we walk through this important topic together, I want

to show you how you can change your thinking *and* transform your life.

In part 1, we'll examine the battle for your mind and how you're really not alone with your thoughts.

In part 2, you'll learn how your brain works and see how to rewire it.

In part 3, you'll discover how to reframe your thinking and redesign your mind around new thoughts.

And in part 4, you'll become equipped to identify your mental triggers and to overcome them through prayer and praise.

Following each chapter, you'll find an exercise that will lead toward the renewal of your mind.

Then, at the end of the book, we'll envision your life ahead. You will see how you can live free of anxiety and negativity while also experiencing the joy and peace that come from knowing God and living in his truth.

If you're skeptical, that's okay. Believe me, I get it. We've all tried unsuccessfully to change bad habits and force our runaway trains of thought back onto the right tracks. But this time you're not alone. You are about to discover that God will team up with you to transform your thinking. And I'll be your guide to walk with you as you start this journey.

With God's help, you *can* transform your mind.

You can stop believing the lies that hold you back.

You can end the vicious cycle of thoughts that are destructive to you and others.

You can allow God to renew your mind by saturating you with his unchanging truth.

You can let his thoughts become your thoughts.

Take it from a guy who survived his teen years but could have done so much better: Our lives are always moving in the direction of our strongest thoughts. What we think will shape who we become.

If you agree with that proposition—and remember, both the Bible and modern science say it's true—then it's time to change your thinking so God can change your life. Doing this work now will only serve you better into adulthood and into your future. Let's get back up on our bikes and ride this out together.

the replacement principle

Remove the Lies, Replace with Truth

God has not given us a spirit of fear, but of power and of love and of a sound mind.

—2 Timothy 1:7 NKJV

perception is *reality*

I love a good prank. You might think that pastors aren't allowed to prank people, but when we do it, it's holy pranking. That's allowed.

Of course, there are rules to a good prank. First, the people you prank should be the type of people who would appreciate the joke. Second, no people or property should be damaged in the prank. Third, you've got to be ready for some kind of return prank if your victim finds out it was you.

There are some classic pranks out there: replacing Oreo cream with toothpaste, attaching googly eyes to everything, and swapping the Pull and Push signs on doors. Seriously, watching people experience these things is hilarious.

One of my favorite pranks was years ago, when I locked my buddy Kevin in a closet at my church. Kevin was on the church staff, and we all used to play capture the flag in the church offices.

I tend to get to work early, and one day as I showed up

around seven o'clock and began walking to my office, my Spidey sense went off. Something wasn't right. Suspecting a threat, I threw open a closet door to find Pastor Kevin hiding. I don't know if he had spent the entire night in there, but his plan was to wait patiently for a surprise attack at go time.

But thanks to my superhero ability to detect danger, I thwarted his plan. I was so excited that I slammed the door shut, wedged my foot against the bottom, and yelled triumphantly, "You're going to spend the day in that closet, Kevin!"

I grabbed a chair to secure my prisoner. Chuckling maniacally, I said, "I'm putting a chair under the doorknob!" But no matter how hard I tried, I couldn't get a chair to fit. And because I couldn't move my foot from the door, there was nothing I could do to lock Kevin in the closet. Fortunately for me, I realized he didn't know that. He believed me. So with all the fake confidence I could muster, I sold it. "There's now a chair under the doorknob, Kevin. You can't get out!"

Well, what did Kevin do? More like what did he *not* do. He never tried to open the door! He just believed me and stayed put.

Eventually Kevin started playfully shouting, "Lemme out! Lemme out! Please, lemme out! I don't want to spend the day in here. Lemme out!"

I couldn't stop laughing. The door was unlocked. All he had to do was turn the handle and push, and he would be free. But he stayed in the closet till I finally got over my laughter and let him out.

Have you ever felt locked up or taken captive? Maybe you feel trapped into thinking you aren't worthwhile. Or that you won't be able to make anything of yourself. Or that no one would ever want to be in a relationship with you. These feelings can be as real and smothering as being trapped in a closet . . . but are you *truly* trapped?

If you think you're trapped, if you believe there's a lock on the door, you've bought into a lie. And it is the lie, nothing else, that is holding you back. If you can spot the lie, you can remove it. You can replace it with the truth and be free. Getting out of your self-imposed prison is a simple two-step process:

- ► Remove the lie.
- ► Replace it with truth.

But the struggle in this process is very real and very hard, and it can feel like a war is being fought in your life. Because that's exactly what is happening.

The Battle for Your Mind

Picture a battle with two opposing sides. Now imagine that the people on one side don't realize they're involved in a battle. The enemy is attacking and taking them out, picking them off one by one, but they just carry on doing what they're doing.

Hard to imagine, right? I agree. But every day, you are engaged in a battle; are you aware of it? You may not recognize the battle you're in while it's completely messing up your life. Ever wonder why you can't shake a habit? Why you feel like you can't connect with God? Why you lose your temper so easily? Why you make bad decision after bad decision? Why you don't want to do what you don't want to do but you do it anyway? Why you and your parents, teachers, friends, or whoever else fight so much? Why you're consumed with worry, fear, and negativity?

There is a reason why. Your mind is a war zone, and you are under attack. It's critical that you become aware of the fight. You cannot change what you do not confront. If you ignore the battle, you lose the battle. The apostle Paul made this truth clear: "We are not fighting against flesh-and-blood enemies, but against evil rulers and authorities of the unseen world, against mighty powers in this dark world, and against evil spirits in the heavenly places" (Ephesians 6:12 NLT).

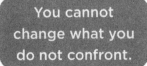

You cannot change what you do not confront.

Your adversary is not your teacher, parent, friend, potential love interest, or neighbor with the deranged dog that is always barking. You may not realize it, but the one you are fighting against is your spiritual enemy, the devil. Sound too extreme? That's exactly what your enemy wants. There is an old saying that goes, "The greatest trick the devil ever pulled was convincing the world he doesn't exist." Satan doesn't want you to believe in him, so he works subtly. He knows that if you ignore him, he can invade your mind without ever triggering your defenses. He can plant seeds of doubt, confusion, worry, depression, and anxiety that will continue to grow.

Satan is your unseen enemy whose mission is to "steal and kill and destroy" (John 10:10), stop you (1 Thessalonians 2:18), and devour you (1 Peter 5:8). Satan despises you with more hatred than you can imagine. He wants to keep you from God and from the life God has for you. He wants to keep you from the close relationships you need most. He wants to rob you of inner joy and abiding peace. He wants to strip you of the fulfillment you could have in knowing you are making a difference with your life.

So how does he do this?

Simple. He lies. Satan is a deceiver, and his strategy to defeat you is to persuade you to believe his lies. Jesus warned us, "There is no truth in him. When he lies, he speaks his native language, for he is a liar and the father of lies" (John 8:44). I think it's interesting that the only time Satan is called a creator, a father, is here in connection to lies.

Understand this: Satan is your enemy, and every day he is prowling around (1 Peter 5:8), watching you, looking for an opening where you might believe a lie.

If you succeed at something, maybe he can convince you that you don't need God. If you fail, he'll try to brainwash you into thinking you'll always be a failure.

Did you have a great experience with someone? He may suggest a relationship is the only thing that will make you happy, especially if it's the wrong thing for you. Was your experience more of a disaster? He'll whisper that no one will ever like you for who you are.

If you do a nice thing for a difficult person, he'll murmur that you're a pretty great person yourself and really don't need God's grace. If instead you speak harshly to someone, he'll whisper that you're an awful, hateful person whom God could never love.

If you're trying to stay away from porn, he will tell you everyone else is watching it. If you give in to porn, he'll make you feel like you're the only person sick enough to do such a disgusting thing.

Satan is conniving and trying to lock you in a prison of lies.

But you are not his prisoner of war unless you choose to be. Those days can be over. That's your call.

As If a Lie Were True

Have you ever heard someone say you should wait thirty minutes after a meal to go swimming? Or that shaving your hair makes it grow back thicker? That bulls get angry when they see red? That you need to drink at least eight glasses of water per day to be healthy?

How about that it takes seven years for your body to digest gum? Or that if you drop a penny from the top of the Empire State Building, you could kill someone? That your hair and fingernails will continue to grow after you die?

Guess what! None of these things are true, but a lot of people still believe them. Whole generations of kids had to wait a half hour after lunchtime just to swim, but they didn't need to! When a lie is believed to be true, it will affect your life as if it were true.

Missing some swimming time isn't a big deal, but what if you believe significant lies that have serious implications? What if you buy into the lie that you'll never be good enough? Or that you made too many mistakes? Or that God doesn't really care about you? Or that you'll never be able to stop doing what you don't want to do?

One more time, because this point is crucial: a lie believed as truth will affect your life as if it were true.

> A lie believed as truth will affect your life as if it were true.

8

There is a specific lie I have believed for as long as I can remember. Living as if that were true has been one of the biggest limiting forces in my life. For years, my strongest thoughts have always been about my shortcomings. I have always felt inadequate. No matter what anyone else said, my inner voice always screamed, *No matter how hard you try, you'll never measure up.*

Why do I feel that way? Frankly, I'm not sure; I have never not felt that way. It seems self-doubt comes naturally to me, or it would if I was a natural at anything.

Essentially, this voice causes me to live a faithless life.

As I type these words about how we can control our thought life, my mind is racing. As David often wrote in Psalms (Psalm 42:5, for example), I am wrestling with my thoughts. I am battling feelings of overwhelming anxiety because I have said yes to too many things and overcommitted myself again.

Yes, my mind is out of control. I wish I could tell you I'm full of faith as I write this first chapter of the book, but my thoughts are full of fear.

But then I come back to what I know is true. And what is true is the point of this book.

I swat at the swarm of thoughts flitting around my head and remember that I am not a victim of my own mind. I have power over my thoughts. I am not captive to them. With God's help, I can make them captive to me.

While I know those truths, at the same time the reality is that I am a struggling thought warrior who has battled insecurity, negativity, fear, and anxiety most of my life. The battles don't stop. Reading this book won't instantly solve the situations you face. The goal, especially for where you are in life, is to give you some tools, some weapons for the battles ahead.

• • •

Midway through college, something dramatic happened to me. Jesus changed my life. By God's grace, he found me and saved me.

Soon I was being so transformed by my relationship with Christ that, while still very new in my faith, I sensed God calling me to be a pastor. (Way before pastors could wear cool shoes and have more Instagram followers than church members.)

As God was building my faith, I felt him telling me I could make a difference in the world through his church. All my childhood insecurities and teenage self-doubts were being eclipsed by glimpses of hope. What do I mean? Well, here's a little backstory for context:

When I was growing up, my family couldn't afford name-brand clothes, so my mother bought used name brand things at garage sales, cut the logos off, and sewed them onto my generic shirts.

I felt fake.

In second grade, I discovered I was color-blind. Not only could I not match my fake name-brand shirts to my no-name pants, I would never see the beauty of this world as others could.

I felt defective.

In a spelling bee with my classmates, I misspelled Mississippi. We had learned a song teaching us how to spell the word. And every time an *i* appears after the M, there's only one of them and two of everything else. How could I possibly misspell Mississippi?

I felt stupid.

In fifth grade, a girl named Tiffany dumped me for a guy named Brian. Her reason? Brian had a motorcycle. I only had a moped. (Yes, twelve-year-olds in my small town drove motor-cycles and mopeds. These were different times.)

I felt lame.

My father played minor league baseball. He was a professional athlete, and I wasn't sure if I could even play in college. I felt inadequate.

These isolated events, along with many others, formed my perception of myself into the reality I would carry into my newfound faith as a young adult.

I felt I wasn't good enough.

So I learned to play it safe and avoid risks at all costs. I felt that, given any opportunity, I would fail. I quietly came to define success as just not failing.

Chances are good you have your own set of lies to deal with. Any of these sound familiar?

- I am invincible.
- No one cares about me.
- I am the center of the universe.
- I am missing out on all the fun.
- I am destined to be famous.
- Everyone is watching me all the time.
- This is the best time of my life. Everything will be downhill from here.
- Everyone else has it figured out.
- Everyone else has it better than me.
- What others think about me is more important than anything else.
- No one could possibly like me because I'm too fat, too thin, too ugly, too whatever.

- ► No one, especially my parents, can understand what I'm going through.
- ► I will always be alone.
- ► Things can never get better.
- ► I'm not capable of changing.
- ► Others wouldn't love me if they knew what I've done.

The lies I believed nearly derailed my future in ministry. How are the lies you believe holding you back?

Not Good Enough

Only weeks after putting my faith in Jesus, I tried to teach my first Bible study to a group of young guys in a little church in Ada, Oklahoma. Afterward, the leader of the youth group said, "Well, I guess teaching the Bible is not your gift, is it?"

Three years later I finally got up the nerve to try teaching the Bible again, after being asked to preach my first sermon. After the service, as I stood at the door saying goodbye to church members, an older gentleman looked at me with a raised brow and remarked, "Nice try." Nice try?!

The next lady in line asked if I had any other skills besides being a preacher and then made a weak attempt to encourage me to keep my options open. Seriously, that really happened. Immediately, all those childhood memories met up with my teenage memories. They joined forces with the rejections from the church, forming an avalanche of negative thoughts that crashed over me, engulfing me. The voices roared loudly, *You aren't enough! You will never be enough! You will never measure up!*

And then the final judgment was delivered: *You . . . don't . . . have . . . what it takes!*

Driving home in my red Geo Prizm, I felt dejected, embarrassed, confused, and angry. Devastated. *How can I explain to my wife that I didn't make the cut? How can I face my pastor? My friends? My classmates? The church where I serve?* The tears flowed as every possible negative thought played on repeat.

But then a strange thing happened.

Suddenly a different voice interrupted the others. God spoke. He spoke to *me*. While not audible, the words somehow seemed louder than any physical voice I had ever heard.

In that moment, my heavenly Father said, "You are not who others say you are. You are who *I* say you are. And I say you are called to ministry."

> "You are not who others say you are. You are who *I* say you are."

While that was of course one of the most powerful moments of my life and a massive turning point, I wasn't suddenly healed of my negative thinking or delivered from believing every lie I'd told myself while growing up. The patterns were still there. The consequences were still ingrained. But I began to realize God had a very different way for me to think and a much healthier way for me to think of myself. I realized he was offering me a choice of either continuing to believe my lies or accepting his truth about me.

That's the beauty of allowing God to master our minds: he gives us a new path, a new way to think, but we have to get on board, agree, and cooperate with him.

I don't know what you envision for your future, whether you want to be a pastor, a teacher, an influencer, an entrepreneur, a content creator, a rockstar-sports-idol-comedian hybrid, or someone who washes cars for a living. If God has placed a calling in your heart, he'll give you what it takes to achieve it. When you place your future in God's hands, your way may take you through some demoralizing experiences (I still can't believe that older gentleman told me, "Nice try!"). Don't stop moving forward! Believing the devil's lies will stop you from getting where God wants you to be.

Lie Detection

But how do you recognize the devil's lies? How can you overcome the negative messages you adopted in your earliest days? Start by asking yourself this question: *What unhealthy and destructive conclusions do I believe about myself and my place in the world?*

Satan's strategy to win the battle for your mind is getting you to believe lies. If you believe a lie, it will hold you back from doing what God's calling you to do.

The lie will keep you living in shame from the past, when God wants to set you free for a better future.

The lie will keep you from living with joy and freedom and confine you to a less-than existence.

Living your life by a lie is a lot like believing the door is locked when it isn't (like my friend Kevin). Freedom is waiting for you, but you first have to commit to some personal lie detection to experience the abundant life Jesus came and died to give you. That leads us to our first exercise.

EXERCISE 1

your thought *audit*

An audit is an official inspection of a company's finances by some outside agency in order to see if the company is healthy. A "thought audit" is an inspection of your thoughts by your own brain to see if your thoughts are healthy. Do you ever find yourself thinking things like:

- ▶ I can't change. Even if I try, I'll always be stuck.
- ▶ Everyone else is doing fine. I'm just broken.
- ▶ No one really loves me. And if they knew the real me, they'd definitely not want to be in my life.
- ▶ I'm not good at relationships. When we start to grow closer, I always do something to mess things up.
- ▶ I don't like the way I look. I don't see how anyone else could either.
- ▶ I can't get close to God. I'm sure it's my fault. There must be something about me that keeps me from experiencing God like others do.
- ▶ When I look at what others post on social media, I feel like my life sucks.

If you think you can't do something, you probably won't. If, on the other hand, you think you can, odds are you will. That's cognitive behavior therapy (CBT) in action. The same is true with your problems. If you dwell on them, they will overwhelm you. But if you look for solutions, you will find some.

If you feel like a victim, you'll think like a victim, and the direction of your life could be one of misery. But if you believe that by the power of Christ you can overcome, then with his help you can. Consider this:

- ▶ Who you are today is a result of your thoughts in the past.
- ▶ Who you become in the future will reflect what you think about today.

Whether it's self-doubts or worrying or responding poorly to a bad day or a tough season in life, we all wrestle with negative thoughts that try to hijack our emotions and decisions.

The goal of this exercise is to help you think about what you think about.

Let's conduct a thought audit. Hit pause for a moment and prepare your mind. Focus on your honest answers. The two parts of this exercise could begin the process of you changing your mind.

Part 1: Inventory

As you go through a normal day, take stock of your thoughts. Write them down or type them into the notes app on your phone. Trust me, if you really want to change, you need to invest the time to figure out what you are regularly thinking. Be honest. Don't lie to yourself about the lies you tell yourself.

Think about how your day typically goes. Are you more negative in the morning but usually fine by dinnertime? Or the opposite? Do you tend to bring negative thinking home with you after school? Or do you manage to leave it there? Consider all the dynamics and patterns of your day. Pray and ask God to show you anything he wants you to see. Ask him for wisdom so you can understand how you think.

Once you see your thoughts in black and white, you can begin to work on your thought life. Jesus said the truth sets us free, but first we must reveal the truth.

Part 2: Audit

Here are twenty questions to help you analyze what you regularly think. I've broken down the questions into two categories: defense (protection from the Enemy) and offense (growth toward God). Write down your honest answers. When you're done, compare your defense and offense. This little quiz will help you see your thoughts and work on real change.

On a typical day:

Defense:
▶ Are my thoughts tearing me down?

▶ Do I think worried thoughts?

▶ Does my self-talk cause me to shrink back in fear?

▶ Do my thoughts cause me to keep people at a distance?

▶ Are my unhealthy thoughts keeping me from the life I want?

▶ Are my unhealthy thoughts keeping me from the life God wants for me?

▶ Are my thoughts negative, toxic, or mean to myself?

▶ Does my inner voice tell me I'm helpless or that life is hopeless?

▶ Do I find myself skeptical of others?

▶ Do I lean toward imagining worst-case scenarios?

Offense:
▶ Are my thoughts building me up?

▶ Do I think peaceful thoughts?

▶ Does my self-talk inspire me to try new things?

▶ Do my thoughts help me get closer to others?

▶ Do my thoughts reflect my faith?

▶ Are my thoughts God-honoring?

▶ Do my thoughts reflect my hope in Christ?

▶ Do they inspire me to believe I can make a difference in the world?

▶ Do they equip me to become more like Jesus?

▶ Do my thoughts connect to the vision God has for my life?

Remember, the goal is to think about what you think about. You can use this information as we move forward to help you take practical steps in winning the battle in your mind. As we continue, we will get to some answers that deal with the truth you have revealed in this exercise. Be encouraged. You are one step closer to changing your thinking and believing what God says about you!

becoming a
thought warrior

The teacher for our advanced thoughtology course will be the apostle Paul.

Paul wrote more books in the Bible's New Testament than any other author. He was a Roman citizen and one of the top Jewish religious leaders, a strange mix for an individual during his time. Paul's dramatic conversion to Christianity can be found in Acts 9:1–22.

In person, Paul wasn't a very impressive person. Second Corinthians 10:10 says, "For some say, 'His letters are weighty and forceful, but in person he is unimpressive and his speaking amounts to nothing.'" But what he lacked in physical presence, Paul made up for in his understanding of how God can use the broken people of this world to act with the power of God. He's exactly the kind of teacher we need to teach us the biblical way to win the battle in our minds.

Incredible as it is to consider, Paul wrote some of his teachings while in prison. And yes, his door was actually locked. Yet even though his body was behind bars, Paul's mind was still free. How? He had taken his thoughts captive long before he entered a jail cell. He knew two truths that we also need to know:

1. The battle for your life is won or lost in your mind.
2. Your thoughts *will* control you, so you have to control your thoughts.

Paul had not always been a thought warrior. Check out how he described himself in Romans 7:15–24:

> I do not understand what I do. For what I want to do I do not do, but what I hate I do. And if I do what I do not want to do, I agree that the law is good. As it is, it is no longer I myself who do it, but it is sin living in me. For I know that good itself does not dwell in me, that is, in my sinful nature. For I have the desire to do what is good, but I cannot carry it out. For I do not do the good I want to do, but the evil I do not want to do—this I keep on doing. Now if I do what I do not want to do, it is no longer I who do it, but it is sin living in me that does it.
>
> So I find this law at work: Although I want to do good, evil is right there with me. For in my inner being I delight in God's law; but I see another law at work in me, waging war against the law of my mind and making me a prisoner of the law of sin at work within me. What a wretched man I am!

That does not sound like a guy who has mastered his

thoughts. It sounds like a guy who's out of control and helpless to change. *This is the guy who's supposed to teach us how to think? Get out of here, Groeschel!*

But check out how Paul describes himself in Philippians 4:12: "I have learned the secret of being content in any and every situation." Now, that *does* sound like a guy who has mastered his thoughts.

Paul's change encourages me because my thought life can be out of control. I despair. I obsess. I can be confused. Sometimes I feel overwhelmed. It's like I'm in a confrontation with myself, and I'm losing.

Honestly, we're all a bit lost sometimes, right? You try not to worry, but you do. You tell yourself to be positive, but you aren't. You try not to obsess about what others think about you, but you do. Like Paul said, "What I want to do I do not do." The daily battle is so frustrating!

But Paul learned to master his mind. He said he learned a secret. So that means we can too.

How did he win the battle for his mind? How can we? Paul also wrote, "Though we live in the world, we do not wage war as the world does. The weapons we fight with are not the weapons of the world. On the contrary, they have divine power to demolish strongholds. We demolish arguments and every pretension that sets itself up against the knowledge of God, and we take captive every thought to make it obedient to Christ" (2 Corinthians 10:3–5).

Notice that Paul used *we* in his statements. Those in a relationship with Christ can experience this change. Let's break down his words and figure this out together.

Declare War

What do you know about war? It seems like there's always some war going on in the world. Usually, one country fights another one in order to take what they have. Sometimes, one country takes offense at something the other one said or did. In 1776, there was the whole tea party deal and taxation without representation that led to the American Revolution.

And in 1925, a war broke out because of a dog.

The War of the Stray Dog, as it was called later, started along the border of Greece and Bulgaria on October 18, 1925. According to one version of the story, a dog belonging to a Greek soldier ran over the border. When the soldier ran after the dog, the Bulgarian border guards saw a Greek soldier running toward them and shot him. The Greek government demanded a formal apology and compensation for the soldier's family, then when they didn't get it, they invaded Bulgaria and occupied the town of Petrich. Eventually, the League of Nations ordered a cease-fire, but before the incident was finished, over fifty people had been killed. All because of a dog.

Wars may be a common sight in our world, but most of the time they feel distant to those of us in the US. You may know soldiers who have seen action, but the battles mostly happen somewhere else in the world.

But here's the thing: You and I are in a war right now. Not a flesh-and-blood, bullets-and-hand-grenades–type war. This kind is even more insidious because it doesn't feel like it's happening. Life just seems normal.

But we are in a war. One that's happening right above

our eyebrows. It's time to open our eyes, glare at our true opponent—the devil—and declare war.

Paul said, "We do not wage war as the world does" (2 Corinthians 10:3).

But the problem is that many Christians don't wage war at all. Satan is assaulting us with negative thoughts. He's delivering blows of deception and bombarding us with lies. Too often, we're oblivious to the attacks and therefore don't fight back.

As a result, our lives are not what we want, and we numb ourselves to reality. We long for more but settle for less. We keep ourselves too busy and distracted. For example, have you found yourself

- ▸ buying things because they offer a distraction from how you're feeling?
- ▸ attempting to impress people in order to fill some mysterious, inner, endless void inside?
- ▸ scrolling mindlessly on social media to avoid thinking about or doing something (and telling yourself you don't feel left out, left behind, and unimportant as you compare your life with everyone else's highlight reels)?

We do our best to pretend we are happy while a war rages around us. And as a result, we are losing battle after battle.

When we don't fight, the enemy wins. Neutrality doesn't work for long.

The United States took a while to engage in World War II. We spent the first years maintaining a neutral position. We believed that because the war was "over there," it wasn't impacting our lives. Eventually, it became clear that Hitler and the Axis powers would not stop, and the freedom of the entire world was hanging in the balance. When the Japanese bombed our naval base at Pearl Harbor, that provocation was the final straw.

Finally, the US entered the war. On D-Day, we joined with other Allied forces as 150,000 troops stormed the beaches of Normandy. The Germans had set about four million land mines to protect the beach from such an invasion. They also rained down gunfire on our men. The sacrifices that day were enormous. Thousands of lives were lost. But the engagement was necessary because there was no other way to defeat evil.

To win the battle for our minds, we must engage, because there is no other way for us to defeat evil. The days of being neutral must be over.

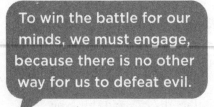

To win the battle for our minds, we must engage, because there is no other way for us to defeat evil.

A few years ago, I began to feel stuck. My thoughts were out of control. I would work on my message for the church, thinking, *Last week's message wasn't good enough, and this one won't be either. I just don't have what it takes. I'm not good enough. I'm not sure I can keep this up. I don't know why people even come to this church.*

If I poured more energy into being a better pastor, I felt like I was failing as a husband and dad. If I gave my best to my family, I was sure I was letting God down and failing the people in my church. Inside my mind, land mines were everywhere, and I was dodging bullets.

Have you ever felt like this? Like if you try harder at school, your extracurricular activities will suffer? Or if you put in more effort at tennis, your grades will slip? Or if you want to spend time with your friends, your family will get mad at you? Like you are stuck, while simultaneously sliding backward, and nothing is getting better? And you're left feeling that maybe it can't?

For me, it was feelings of weakness. My thoughts always returned to how I wasn't measuring up, and I knew they were leading me to a place I did not want to go. Finally, I decided I'd had enough. I had to do something. It was time to win the battle for my mind.

It was time to declare a thought war.

For about two years, my mind was my number one priority of prayer. I read so many books on the topic that I lost count. I also received counseling from a psychologist and confided in trusted friends and mentors.

I discovered some tools and put them into practice. I did mental exercises and worked toward two main goals: retrain my thought patterns and change the trajectory of my life.

Bottom line: I knew that if I ignored the battle any longer, I'd lose it.

So I changed my thinking, and that decision changed everything.

Destroying the Stronghold

The lies we believe and base our lives upon are strongholds. Paul said, "The weapons we fight with . . . have divine power to demolish strongholds" (2 Corinthians 10:4). So we need to demolish those lies that harm us.

The word *stronghold* is translated from the Greek word *ochuroma*, which means "to fortify." In ancient times, a stronghold was a building, a fortress built on top of the highest peak in the city. This citadel was surrounded by a reinforced wall up to twenty feet thick.

In times of war, if the city was attacked, the stronghold was often seen as unapproachable and impenetrable. Political leaders were hidden there so they wouldn't be captured or killed.

Paul compared the lies we believe to those fortresses. Like the walls of the strongholds, our lies have been reinforced over and over to become bigger and stronger. We have believed them for so long, they have become a part of us. We believe our walls protect us. We think they are impenetrable. And yet they often keep the truth unapproachable to us.

We have mental and emotional strongholds—the lies that have a "strong hold" on us.

I told you before about my belief that I could never be enough—not good enough, smart enough, or successful enough. I thought I had to prove I was worthy. You may have read that and thought, *But Craig, you're a pastor. You know the Bible. God tells us that we don't need to be enough. Jesus was enough for us. Craig, you know that God loves you and that's all that matters.* Yes, you would be right. I did know that. I taught that. But deep down I felt like that truth applied to everyone but me.

Knowing those truths was not enough to penetrate the walls of my stronghold. My stronghold kept the truth unapproachable. I still believed the lie that I was not worthy and had to prove myself, and that lie affected my life as if it were true. Yes, even as a pastor who taught others that very truth.

Solomon gave us some very wise counsel to apply to this

battle: "One who is wise can go up against the city of the mighty and pull down the stronghold in which they trust" (Proverbs 21:22).

If you are in a war and attack a city, make sure you take down the stronghold. If you don't take the more difficult action of bringing it down, the city will reestablish itself. The leaders are hiding inside the walls, still very much alive.

For the same reasons, you have to bring down your mental stronghold.

Our word *demolish* is translated from the Greek word *kathaireo*, which means "destruction requiring massive power." The word also means "to lower with violence"—to bring something down with brute strength, as with a wrecking ball.

Regardless of our perceived strength, you and I do not have massive, wrecking ball power. But God does, and he has made it available to us.

Yet again Paul taught us the concept: "I also pray that you will understand the incredible greatness of God's power for us who believe him. This is the same mighty power that raised Christ from the dead" (Ephesians 1:19–20 NLT).

That's incredible! The same power that raised Jesus from the dead is available to you and me.

Wow! Let that truth sink in.

You have supernatural, resurrection, roll-the-stone-away power at hand to change your mind, transform your thoughts, and win the war. If God's power can take Jesus from death to life, then whatever you need can be done for you too. That's the kind of massive power God is offering you. Isn't that encouraging? You've got astonishing power to help you.

Don't Give Up, Look Up

What's your stronghold?

What lie is holding you hostage?

What mistruth keeps you from taking a step of faith?

What wrong thought pattern robs you of living a life of freedom and joy?

Know this: You cannot defeat what you cannot define. You have to identify the lie that has become a stronghold for you. You must realize the negative impact it's had on you and others.

> **You cannot defeat what you cannot define.**

This isn't an easy or fun process. It can be painful to face the truth and recognize the stronghold of lies for what it is. But this is where things start to change for the better.

Do you see how you have become a prisoner of deception, locked up by a lie you believe is true? If you are going to change your life, you have to change your thinking. Demolish your strongholds.

If you want to truly change your life, you cannot just change your behavior. Even if you change your actions for a while, the original issue will just reestablish itself. That's why Christianity has never been about behavior modification; it's about life transformation.

We've all experienced that frustration, right? We get tired of how things aren't working for us, so we make a commitment to start or stop doing something. Start working out, spend less time on our phones, pray more, stop swearing and cursing. Well, for a few weeks it seems to work, and then we go right back to doing what we always do. Why? We haven't gotten to the root of the problem: the lie we believe.

Addressing the problem is attacking the city. Identifying and destroying the lie is pulling down the stronghold. Both are necessary to win the war.

To do both and experience success, we need God's power. We cannot have victory without his strength and support.

I have good news that might sound like bad news at first. You ready?

You don't have what it takes to win the war. Neither do I.

You know it because you've tried. You've tried to change your thinking, tried to change your life. You've done everything you can, but you always end up back in the same place. You keep doing what you don't want to do and not doing what you want to do, just like Paul. You keep falling down and falling short. I get it. Been there, done that.

All the trying and failing and falling can lead to a place where we feel like giving up.

What's the problem? The power you need is a power you don't possess. Relying on your own power is self-help, and self-help goes only skin-deep.

You have a devious spiritual enemy. You have reinforced strongholds. What stands against you is formidable. Fighting in your own power is like attacking Thanos with a flyswatter.

Admitting that you need a power you don't possess is vital, even though it may be difficult. I know it has been for me. If you've been taught to be an independent, self-reliant individual, confessing you don't have what it takes might feel like weakness. But it's not. It takes real strength to admit, *I can't do this on my own. I need power greater than I possess.*

Once, after a blizzard, I tried to shovel a path to our cars, to get enough snow off our driveway to back them out. In two solid, backbreaking hours, I had cleared a pathway big enough for a small squirrel to walk through. Just as my wife was about to call 9 1 1 to save me from permanent frostbite damage, a neighbor from down the street drove by on his tractor. (Yes, my neighbor drives a tractor. I live in Oklahoma.) In a matter of minutes, because of the power he possessed, my helpful neighbor had cleared our entire driveway.

We tend to fight our battles with shovel power. But we need tractor power. We need a power we don't possess. We have to ask for and receive help.

Have you ever heard insanity defined as *doing the same thing but expecting different results?* If you have tried with everything you have and it hasn't worked, stop. Don't keep doing the same thing. You'll get the same results. If you feel like you just have to admit defeat and stop trying, don't do that either. Because you'll keep living the same life.

Don't give up. Look up.

Look up because you have a gracious, generous God who has the power you need and wants to share it with you.

To bring down your strongholds, it's time to go up. As a child of God, you have access to everything that belongs to your heavenly Father. So look up, go up, and access the power God has that you need to remove lies and replace them with truth. Ask him to show you the lies that you have believed for too long. Tell him you want your mind to be filled with his truths instead of the devil's lies. And then thank him for hearing you.

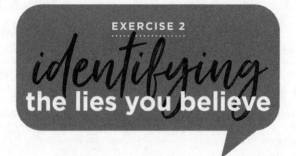

EXERCISE 2

identifying
the lies you believe

In the first exercise, you took an honest inventory and made an audit of how you tend to think on a regular basis. In this exercise, we're going to dive deeper and get more specific.

I want to repeat a crucial section of this chapter that needs to be connected to this exercise:

What lie is holding you hostage?
What mistruth keeps you from taking a step of faith?
What wrong thought pattern robs you of living a life of freedom and joy?

Know this: You cannot defeat what you cannot define. You have to identify the lie that has become a stronghold for you. You must realize the negative impact it's had on you and others.

Use these questions to trigger your thoughts; it's now time to define the lies you've been believing, identify the strongholds in your life, and face their negative impact.

This is important, so take the time necessary to disconnect from the world around you before beginning this exercise. Put down the phone. Put a sign on the door to your bedroom if needed. Once you are free from all distractions, focus on identifying the specific lies you believe. I have given you plenty of examples of lies I've believed and have had to address, both old ones and new ones. Make your statements personal and straightforward, as in, "I believe I am not good enough." Get them out. Write them down.

My lies:

old lies, *new truth*

If we are going to demolish our strongholds, we have to recognize the power that lies have over us. Think of it this way:

There is a large, shaggy-haired, lumbering dog—let's call him Max—who will not leave the yard. A car drives by. Max loves to chase cars. The thought of grabbing one by the bumper and wrestling the beast into submission makes him drool. Max wants to give chase so badly, but he just sits in the yard.

Then two boys start playing catch in the street. The ball rolls right to the edge of Max's yard. He desperately wants to get the ball and run from the boys. But he doesn't. One of them teases the dog. "What's the matter, Max? Afraid of the ball?" Max wants to bite the brat, but his tormentor is just outside the yard.

A cat walks down the street. Max cannot imagine the nerve of this cat. He knows they are evil and that they are on this earth only to do wreak havoc. Max wants to attack, to bring a hailstorm of violence onto this feline's life. Yet he cannot.

Why?

An invisible electric fence lines the perimeter of his yard.

This type of fence puts out a little invisible beam, and when an unsuspecting dog crosses the line—zap! He gets a small jolt of electricity. The first time, the dog is confused. He tries to leave the yard again—zap. Another painful little sting. If the dog is stubborn, or just dumb, he might try a third time. After that, he's learned his lesson. He knows he will never be able to leave the yard again.

Max's owners have an invisible electric fence.

Actually, Max's owners *used* to have an electric fence. They bought one, set it up, and turned it on. Max was shocked several times. After a time though, Max's owners decided to return the electric fence to the store.

Several years have passed since they owned the fence. Even still, Max will not leave the yard. Why? He thinks he can't. His shaggy dog brain has been trained to believe he can't. In his mind he is a prisoner, missing out on the life he wants to live. He associates life outside the boundaries of his yard with pain. The magical place where cars can be caught, balls can be stolen, and the evil mission of cats can be thwarted is just out of reach. He has no idea that the only thing keeping him constrained is a lie he believes.

You laugh, but is it possible you may be more like Max than you think?

Are you also a prisoner, missing out on the life you want but believe you can never have? You crave close relationships but are paralyzed by the fear of rejection. You want to try something new but assume you are destined to fail. You worry that people only like you because you're funny or good-looking or whatever, so you try to only show that one thing. You dream of losing weight and exercising but feel resigned to fail yet again. You want to change but think you never can.

Why?

You are constrained by a lie, something that doesn't exist. The Enemy has arranged enough hurtful circumstances in key places of your life, in which you got just enough jolt—a bit of a shock, a sting of pain to your heart—that you have decided trying even one more time is just not worth the risk. What makes it worse is that the number of places where you have stopped trying is growing ever larger.

As we've discussed, the greatest weapon in Satan's arsenal is the lie. Perhaps his only weapon is the lie. The first glimpse we have of the devil in the Bible, we see him deceiving Adam and Eve in the garden. He created doubt in Eve's mind by asking her:

> "Did God really say, 'You must not eat from any tree in the garden'?"
>
> The woman said to the serpent, "We may eat fruit from the trees in the garden, but God did say, 'You must not eat fruit from the tree that is in the middle of the garden, and you must not touch it, or you will die.'"
>
> "You will not certainly die," the serpent said to the woman. "For God knows that when you eat from it your eyes will be opened, and you will be like God, knowing good and evil."
>
> —GENESIS 3:1–5

What Satan did in the garden back then is the exact same thing he will attempt to do in your life today.

In 2 Corinthians 11:3, our thoughtology teacher Paul said, "I am afraid that just as Eve was deceived by the serpent's cunning, your minds may somehow be led astray from your sincere and pure devotion to Christ."

Satan will whisper accusing questions and deceptive statements. He schemes to twist your mind, because if he can, he then

- diverts you from your purpose,
- distracts you from God's voice,
- destroys your potential.

If he can get you to believe a lie, your life will be affected as if that lie were true.

Unfortunately, Satan's lies are easy to believe. Why? Part of the reason is that because of sin, we have a flawed internal lie detector. God warned us:

- "The heart is deceitful above all things and beyond cure" (Jeremiah 17:9).
- "There is a way that appears to be right, but in the end it leads to death" (Proverbs 14:12).

That's definitely the problem, so what's our solution? How do we access God's power to stop Satan's lies? How can we demolish his strongholds in our lives?

If Satan's primary weapon is lies, then our greatest counterweapon is the truth of God's Word. Not just reading the Bible but learning to wield Scripture as a divine weapon. God wants us to view his Word that way. See how Hebrews 4:12 offers a direct solution to the warning of Jeremiah 17:9: "The word of God is alive and active. Sharper than any double-edged sword,

> If Satan's primary weapon is lies, then our greatest counter-weapon is the truth of God's Word.

it penetrates even to dividing soul and spirit, joints and marrow; it judges the thoughts and attitudes of the heart."

In Ephesians 6:17, Paul's legendary armor of God passage, the Word of God is called "the sword of the Spirit." God's Word was the first weapon I learned to use to remove lies and replace them with truth, changing both my thinking and my life. "Do not conform to the pattern of this world, but be transformed by the renewing of your mind" (Romans 12:2).

The second half of that sentence is in the passive voice, meaning it is not something we do but instead something that is done to us. The good news is that God is ready to renew our minds by leading us to "a knowledge of the truth" (2 Timothy 2:25). Why? So we can "come to [our] senses and escape from the trap of the devil, who has taken [us] captive to do his will" (v. 26). "Then," as Jesus said, "[we] will know the truth, and the truth will set [us] free" (John 8:32).

Turning the Tables

We've been held captive by the lies we believe, so now we are going to take those lies captive. Capturing the lie is not so easy, because first we must realize the lie. How? Here is our three-step process:

1. Identify the problem.
2. Ask probing questions.
3. Pinpoint the lie.

This process can work because while you don't know the lies you believe are lies, you do know that the problems you experience are problems. Problems are easier to identify, so if you're willing to ask some probing questions, you will be able to pinpoint the lies that are holding you captive.

I'll show you how this works with some examples.

Let's say your problem is going physically farther with boys or girls than you know is good at this point in your life. Things start innocently enough, but one thing leads to another. Holding hands turns to kissing. Kissing turns to more.

Maybe you feel pressured but shrug it off because you want to make the other person happy. Besides, it feels good on some level, right? You are pretty sure everyone your age is doing the same things. And what would happen if you stopped now? You worry you'll lose your relationship—even if you know that a relationship based only on physical affection is probably not worth having. Then you wonder if you actually *are* going farther than everyone else. What will they say about you if they find out? So you keep going down the path you are on because at least the person you are with is as guilty as you are and they still seem to like you. All the while, you know this isn't right.

You have identified a problem. Now ask probing questions like:

▸ Why am I doing this?

- ► When did this start?
- ► How does this make me feel?
- ► Is fear driving this?
- ► If so, what am I afraid of?
- ► Is there a certain trigger that prompts this behavior?
- ► If so, why do I find it so hard to stop?

As you ask your probing questions, pray for God's help to pinpoint the lie at the root of your behavior. Perhaps you'll realize that you've equated love with physicality when that's only one expression of it. That gave the devil an opportunity to deceive you into believing the lie, "If I just go along with what my boyfriend or girlfriend wants, I'll be happier," or, "This is just part of being popular," or, "If it feels good, how can it be bad?" The good feelings are extremely short lived, yet you keep coming back to them—and going farther than you want to—because a lie believed as true will affect your life as if it were true.

Perhaps the problem you identify is a self-destructive habit or addiction. Maybe you regularly sit down and eat a half gallon of ice cream. You wouldn't be alone in that practice (my weakness is mint chocolate chip), whether it's ice cream or chips or candy or some other not-meant-to-be-eaten-in-huge-quantities-all-the-time treat. According to the National Center for Health Statistics (part of the US Centers for Disease Control and Prevention), the prevalence of obesity in the US for twelve- to nineteen-year-olds has risen from 5 percent between 1976 and 1980 to 14.8 percent in 2000 to 21.2 percent in 2018.[1] And like us when we turn to food for comfort, that statistic keeps getting bigger.

Of course, you could struggle with the opposite of obesity too. Body image struggles are incredibly common. According to a popular study, by age thirteen, 53 percent of American girls are "unhappy with their bodies." By the time girls reach seventeen, this number rises to 78 percent.[2] But it isn't just girls, right? Guys struggle too. And when body image anxiety reaches a certain point, it can lead to an eating disorder. According to the National Institute of Mental Health, 3 percent (one out of every thirty-three) seventeen- and eighteen-year-olds struggle with anorexia nervosa, bulimia nervosa, or binge eating disorder.[3]

Maybe it isn't a food or body image thing for you. Maybe you get home from school and plug straight into the internet, ignoring everyone else physically around you. According to the Kaiser Family Foundation, adolescents from ages eight to eighteen spend an average of seven and a half hours in front of a screen for entertainment each day.[4] That's just the fun time, not including screen time spent on education at school or homework at home. There's all kinds of data suggesting that people who have heavy screen time are less likely to get good grades, get along with their parents, be happy at school, stay out of trouble, and avoid boredom, but that doesn't stop us from turning on the screen and tuning out to avoid the problems caused by staring at screens for hours.

Maybe you can't relax without the help of pills, alcohol, or marijuana. Did you know that even though underage drinking is illegal, findings show that people between the ages of twelve and twenty drink about 4 percent of all alcohol consumed in the United States? And 90 percent of what that age group drinks is part of binge drinking.[5] In addition, about

40 percent of high schoolers have reported using marijuana.[6] Increasingly, teens like you are using prescription medications for non-prescription purposes.

In her book, *The Teenage Brain*, neuroscientist Frances E. Jensen, MD, retold the story of Ian James Eaccarino, a college student who was killed by an accidental overdose of heroin and valium. Ginger Katz, Ian's mom, related the following on the Courage to Speak website:

> "Ian started using tobacco and marijuana in the eighth grade. He was in denial about the problem, minimizing it as so many young people do. I was unaware that he was using drugs, thinking the changes were just adolescent behavior.
>
> Ian became very good at disguising his drug habit. All through high school, he excelled on the baseball team and was the third highest scorer on the lacrosse team. He insisted he was okay, but he really wasn't.
>
> In his senior year of high school, his car was firebombed in the driveway of our home. In retrospect, we realized it was drug related, but at the time, the explanation he gave us made sense. It was all a lie. Drug activity is typically associated with violence and deception.
>
> Nine months before he died, Ian and two friends snorted heroin for the first time. He was a college sophomore at the time. One boy became scared, one became sick—and Ian liked it."[7]

No one sets out to develop an addiction—whether sexual or food or social media likes or heroin—but your brain lights up when you give in to the cravings. The teenage brain is especially susceptible to addictive substances and behaviors. You probably know these are harmful while you do them, but you can't seem to stop. You've uncovered the problematic behavior. Now it's time to ask the probing questions.

- ► What is driving my behavior?
- ► What need do I feel this is meeting?
- ► Does identifying *when* I do this help me understand *why* I do it?
- ► What is different about this habit than others I have been able to quit?

The questions may lead you to the conclusion that a substance you use (yes, even mint chocolate chip ice cream can be a substance) helps relieve stress and gives you a temporary feeling of peace. You may realize something is just providing a momentary endorphin rush that never ends in a good place.

Your first thought might be, *What's wrong with that?* but I'm guessing you already know. God promises to be our refuge, the one who gives us rest, our peace provider. So who might put the idea in your head that God can't do what he promises and that you need to turn to something other than him instead?

> God promises to be our refuge, the one who gives us rest, our peace provider.

Let's say your questions lead you to detect a theme in your life: you seem to sabotage yourself. You let people walk all over you. You don't get the lead in the school musical. In fact, you don't even try out for the musical, because you believe that kind of thing never happens to you. You would love to have a special someone to hang out with, but you are sure you will never find anyone like that—or if you do, they will reject you.

Why? Search your feelings.

You investigate the pattern of self-sabotage, and perhaps you have an epiphany. *I think I'm a victim. I believe I can never win.*

Maybe your problem is that you worry constantly. You are always trying to plan out all the details of your future because you cannot stand not knowing the plan.

Go somewhere you're by yourself, turn off the phone, pray for help in being honest with yourself, and ask probing questions, such as:

- ► When did this start?
- ► Why do I feel this way?
- ► Why do I insist on being in control when I know, deep down, I'm not?
- ► What is the real need I'm trying to meet with this wrong thinking?

Then pinpoint the lie. It could be that you believe God can't really be trusted. You need to be in control, because that is your best bet at getting the life you want. You realize that rather than surrendering yourself to God, you are trying to manipulate him to serve your own purposes.

See how this works?

Allow me to show you how this has played out in my life.

I grew up an overachiever. Not because I was gifted but because I worked myself into the ground trying to hide my faults and compensate for my weaknesses. I completely believed that I had to produce, win, perform, be the best. That these things were needed to be liked, to fit in, to be valuable, to be worth anything.

It was a horrible lie. In fact, it was paralyzing.

If I couldn't be good at something, I wouldn't do it. That kept me away from doing a lot of things I might have enjoyed.

When it came to school, I didn't really have a choice to avoid the things I wasn't naturally good at, so I worked really hard. And even though I got good grades, it wasn't because I was the smartest. It was because I was driven by this paralyzing fear that if I wasn't good enough at school or sports or life, no one would like me.

And that didn't stop with high school. I carried this fear with me through college and into my grown up job and life.

I entered into full-time ministry as a twenty-three-year-old married man. I was also a full-time seminary student. My wife and I started multiplying like rabbits. I worked nonstop. I would go months without taking a single day off. Every day, I was the first one to work and the last one to leave. I went years without taking a real vacation.

For a long time, I believed my work ethic was a God-honoring way to live. One evening, I was working late at the office again. My young daughter Catie called. I promised her I'd be home soon to play with her. Catie replied with sadness, "Daddy, you don't live at home. You live at the office."

As soon as I heard her innocent but honest statement, time stood still. It was hard to breathe. God got my attention through my little girl. I was putting everything that really mattered at risk. What would my life have been like if I had learned to identify Satan's lies in my teens? I'll never know. But when I heard Catie's truthful sadness, I realized I had a problem and had to change.

When you identify a problem, what do you do? You ask probing questions.

So I did. I asked. I prayed. I sought help from a therapist.

Eventually, I pinpointed the lie: I believed my worth was based on what other people thought of me. The problem was I had become a people pleaser.

I believed a lie, and it affected my life as if it were true.

Have these examples raised some red flags in your life?

Is it time for you to identify a problem?

Ask some probing questions?

Pinpoint a lie? Maybe a few?

Remember, you are in a battle. The battle is for your mind. Your entire life, Satan has been trying to bait you so he can entice you with lies that will capture and imprison you. Now it's time to go on the offensive. Time to get God's help to capture the lie.

If you are considering getting some outside help but feel hesitant, I get it. I felt the same way. The thing to remember is, just like in every other area of life, the best way to get better is to get help, to get coaching, to get support. See this as a step to find someone who will help you get better.

If you need help finding someone to talk to, consider asking your pastor, your youth pastor, a teacher, or a trusted friend for advice. Support is always available. From professional counselors to nonprofit organizations that specialize in helping teens, there are people who care about getting you into a better mental and emotional space.

And because I don't know where you are or how you're feeling right now, I want you to know about the 988 Suicide & Crisis Lifeline (formerly known as the National Suicide Prevention Lifeline). It's heartbreaking that suicide is the second leading cause of death for people between ten and twenty-four years old. If you feel lost and hopeless right now, call or text 988 and talk to someone. It's free, confidential, and staffed by people who care.

Only the Truth Can Set You Free

The battle we're in is especially insidious because it's invisible. We can't see our enemy. We don't realize he's the one leading us to believe the lies (which we probably don't even recognize as lies). But there was a time in history when this battle was not invisible, and that provides clear clues about how to wield God's massive power to demolish enemy-occupied strongholds.

In Matthew 4, we read about Jesus, who after his baptism headed into the desert, where he fasted for forty days and nights. At the end of that time, Satan came to Jesus to tempt him.

Because he knew Jesus had to be hungry, Satan told him to turn stones into bread. Just as he did with Adam and Eve, Satan was trying to get Jesus to do something that wasn't part of God's plan for his life. (That's also what Satan does with you.)

Jesus replied, "It is written: 'Man shall not live on bread alone, but on every word that comes from the mouth of God'" (Matthew 4:4), quoting Deuteronomy 8:3.

Satan realized his first plan failed, so he attacked Jesus

from a different angle. (That is also exactly what Satan does with you.) Same method, new try.

The devil took Jesus to the highest point on the temple in Jerusalem and dared him to throw himself off. Satan decided that two can play this game, so he quoted Psalm 91: "It is written: 'He will command his angels concerning you, and they will lift you up in their hands, so that you will not strike your foot against a stone'" (Matthew 4:6). (Yes, Satan knows the Bible too.) He wanted to tempt Jesus to prove he was truly God's Son by trying to force God to show evidence of his love and care.

Jesus stayed on point and simply answered, "Do not put the Lord your God to the test" (Matthew 4:7), quoting Deuteronomy 6:16.

That didn't work either, so Satan tried a different way of burrowing his way into Jesus's thinking. (Again, that is exactly what Satan does with you.)

He brought Jesus to a tall mountain, showed him the kingdoms of the world, and offered to give it all to him if Jesus would just bow down and worship him.

Jesus had now had enough and commanded, "Away from me, Satan!" He then quoted Deuteronomy 6:13: "For it is written: 'Worship the Lord your God, and serve him only'" (Matthew 4:10).

Shouldn't we take the same approach Jesus did?

We are going to "take captive every thought to make it obedient to Christ" (2 Corinthians 10:5) by using our process to pinpoint the lie, and then we will replace that lie with the truth that sets us free.

Three times, in three separate instances and temptations,

Jesus exposed Satan's lie and engaged the truth of God's Word that he had been memorizing since he was a young Jewish boy.

The first tool I learned that renewed my mind and transformed my life was the Replacement Principle: Remove the lies, replace with truth. Once you grasp this tool, this weapon, you can begin to use it regularly to change your mind and your life.

> The Replacement Principle: Remove the lies, replace with truth.

Jesus's clear example, detailed for us in Matthew 4, is why it is essential that we know the Bible. As followers of Christ, we prioritize reading the Bible, listen to Bible teaching, join Bible studies, and get God's Word into our hearts so we can wield the sword against the lies of the Enemy.

Let's see how this could work with the examples we considered earlier.

You identified a problem of getting too physical in relationships. You asked probing questions that led you to expose the lie you believed: "If I just go along with what my boyfriend or girlfriend wants, I'll be happier. It doesn't really matter if we're married to enjoy each other because that's not how the world works anymore."

The next step is to replace that lie with God's truth. "Flee from sexual immorality. All other sins a person commits are outside the body, but whoever sins sexually, sins against their own body" (1 Corinthians 6:18).

"Marriage should be honored by all, and the marriage bed kept pure, for God will judge the adulterer and all the sexually immoral" (Hebrews 13:4).

Now write this biblical truth into your own declaration:

"I know that true happiness can only be found in God's presence. When I live for God instead of my physical pleasure or to make someone else happy, I can live guilt-free, and that's better than momentary pleasure. Sex is great as long as it is with the right person at the right time in the right situation" (Psalm 16:11, Romans 13:14).

The problem that plagues you is a self-destructive habit—things like ice cream, alcohol, pills, bad relationships. You captured the lie: you believe you need whatever it is to help relieve stress and give you peace.

What's the truth? Jesus said, "Come to me, all you who are weary and burdened, and I will give you rest. Take my yoke upon you and learn from me, for I am gentle and humble in heart, and you will find rest for your souls. For my yoke is easy and my burden is light" (Matthew 11:28–30).

Your declaration: "I do need help; I need God's help. What I am using may numb me to my problem but does not help me. God tells me to come to him when I am weary, burdened, or overwhelmed. He tells me to 'cast all [my] anxiety on him because he cares for [me]' (1 Peter 5:7), and he promises to be my 'refuge and strength, an ever-present help in trouble' (Psalm 46:1)."

You get the pattern now, but here are a couple more in a concise template:

Lie: "I'm a victim; nothing good ever happens to me."
Truth: "If God is for us, who can be against us? . . . In all these things we are more than conquerors through him who loved us" (Romans 8:31, 37)
Declaration: "God tells me that I am not a victim but a

victor in Christ. I am an overcomer, and 'I can do all this through him who gives me strength'" (Philippians 4:13).

Lie: "God can't really be trusted. I need to be in control of my own life."

Truth: "God demonstrates his own love for us in this: While we were still sinners, Christ died for us" (Romans 5:8).

Declaration: "God loves me more than I love myself. He knows me better than I know myself. He has my best interests in mind, and he can be trusted. If he 'did not spare his own Son, but gave him up for us all—how will he not also, along with him, graciously give us all things?'" (Romans 8:32).

See how this life-transforming tool works? Remove the lie. Replace with truth.

I'll show you how this worked for me, using my confession of overworking.

For years I overachieved and overextended myself in unhealthy ways, just thinking of myself as a hard worker. Finally, I realized that what was driving me wasn't my work ethic but rather a desperate need to win the approval of other people. I wrongly believed my worth was based on what other people thought of me. I had to replace that lie with the truth.

The truth, not just for me but for you, is that our value is based not on what we do but on who made us (Psalm 139:13–16). That's why paintings that may look goofy to me are worth millions of dollars. Because if they were painted by Pablo Picasso, the value is in the hundreds of thousands or millions. So if God made me, I have tremendous value even if I do not have the approval of other people.

The truth, again not just for me but for you, is that our value is based not on how we feel about ourselves but on what someone else will pay for us (1 Peter 1:18–19). That's why a Lamborghini that might not impress you is actually worth three hundred thousand dollars. If someone is willing to pay that price, that's what it's worth. And if God paid the price of his only Son for me, I have infinite value regardless of what other people think of me.

> The truth, not just for me but for you, is that our value is based not on what we do but on who made us (Psalm 139:13–16).

So now whenever I think I need to impress people, I take that thought captive and make it obedient to Christ. The verb tense of "take captive" in the Bible's original language implies a repeated and continuous action. This is not something you do once. This is something you will have to do thousands of times in your life, maybe dozens of times a day. The definition of a principle is a decision you make once and then live by.

Believe me, I am not saying this process is easy. I am still tempted to believe the lies, and I suspect you will be also. But these battles between our lies and God's truth are worth fighting! Because waging war as I have been training you to do in these pages is what will change your mind, redeem your thinking, and ultimately revolutionize your life.

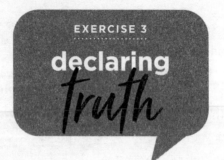

EXERCISE 3

declaring *truth*

This exercise builds on your work in exercise 2. Look back and use the lies you wrote there for this session. The goal is to take what God is revealing to you and build helpful tools to use in your life.

To do so, I want to give you the place and space to work out your lies, truths, and declarations. In this chapter, we walked through several examples in detail. Now it's time for you to work through your own. For the truth in this book to truly change your life, you will have to put in the personal work that I have had to do over these past years and still do. The last thing you or I want is for your life to look the same after you finish this book as it did when you started.

Dig in, go deep, and allow God to show you his truth in his Word. You will need to find truths in the Bible you can use as your own personal truths to replace the lies you are believing.

Lie:

Truth:

Declaration:

Lie:

Truth:

Declaration:

Lie:

Truth:

Declaration:

Lie:

Truth:

Declaration:

PART

2

the rewire principle

Rewire Your Brain,
Renew Your Mind

*Do not conform to the pattern of
this world, but be transformed by the
renewing of your mind. Then you will be
able to test and approve what God's will
is—his good, pleasing and perfect will.*

—Romans 12:2

crossed wires and
circular ruts

Teens today aren't getting their driver's licenses as early as they did when I grew up. According to Federal Highway Administration studies, the share of eighteen-year-olds across the country who have a driver's license dropped from 71.5 percent in 1996 to an incredibly low 58 percent in 2020.[1] With the rise in walkable communities and services like Uber, teens don't need to have their driver's licenses like they used to.

But you probably still appreciate the need for freedom, the need to be your own person and decide how you want to spend your time and who you want to hang out with. For me, having a car was a step toward freedom.

My first car was a Buick Century. I don't know how much you know about Buicks, so let me fill you in. Buicks have *never* been considered cool by teenagers (or pretty much anyone for that matter). The prime audience for a Buick is a grown-up who wants a smooth ride but can't afford a Cadillac. It's the person for whom words like "dependability" and "sensibility" are highly praised.

But here's the thing about my Buick Century. It wasn't a normal Buick. In the mid to late 1970s, the big decision makers at Buick wanted to compete with the other automakers for a slice of the "muscle car" pie. So they hoped to create a Buick that could hold its own in the street races they knew teens were holding. They created the 1979 Buick Century Turbo Coupe. It had a 3.8-liter turbocharged V-6 engine and produced 175 horsepower and 275 pound-feet of torque—less than a Corvette, but lighter than one too. And just to make sure everyone knew that this Buick wasn't your grandma's Buick, it had a spoiler, said "Turbo Coupe" across the back, and sported majestic eagle stickers (talons out and ready to grab a tree branch and proclaim liberty for all) on the quarter panels just above and behind the front tires.

What color was this miracle of Buick engineering, you ask? C'mon, what color car do you think someone with my unbridled coolness would have? Brown. It could have been red, silver, or medium blue, but no. It was brown. Buick may have called it "dark gold," but we all knew it looked like the inside of a used diaper.

Now let's talk about the sound for a minute. "It is, in a word, loud," said a *Car and Driver* review from back in the day. It was *designed* to be loud. It didn't have mufflers and barely passed the government's noise level tests.[2]

By the time my parents handed the car over to me in 1986, it hadn't gotten any quieter. In order to combat the engine noise, as well as add some level of coolness to my teenage attributes (let's not talk about my shaggy, almost-a-mullet hairstyle and unibrow), I decided to install a thumping sound system to blast my favorite tunes.

I landed myself the coolest used Alpine stereo system I could find. *Yes!* Now I could hear my favorite bands in full surround, supersonic, we-will-rock-you, make-my-ears-bleed, rock-your-face-off, I-can't-drive-fifty-five, we-built-this-city-on-rock-and-roll, quadraphonic super bass sound.

There was only one problem. Spending all my money buying the stereo system meant I couldn't afford to have it professionally installed. No, not a problem; I could install it! How hard could it be?

But I was and still am technically challenged. I can barely install a piece of bread into a toaster. Putting in my new car stereo in those pre–"watch a YouTube video to learn how to do anything" days was a nightmare. After working on the install all day, I still couldn't get the thing to work. Finally, by evening, with the eagles on my car soaring under the moon in the dark of night, I got my Alpine stereo to work! As the sun went down, the volume went up. Praise God from whom all blessings flow; he put the rock in my roll!

But the next morning, tragedy stuck. When I started my car and pushed the power button on my Alpine, nothing happened. My self-installed, only-gently-used stereo didn't work. I pressed the button again. Pressed it harder. Nothing. *Why?!*

I could not get it to work all day long. Then, magically, that night it started working again. The next morning, dead. That night, mysteriously back to life again. Day after day, the same thing. During the day, nothing. Every night, perfect.

I figured out the pattern, but I could not find the problem.

Some of you who are smarter than I was in 1986 have diagnosed the issue, haven't you?

Why would my car stereo work only at night?

Well, what electrical device do you tend to turn on at night in your car? Bingo!

I had crossed the wires.

Instead of wiring my car stereo to the proper source of power, I had wired it to my headlights. I could crank my tunes only if the lights were on. So for the rest of the life of my 1979 Buick Century Turbo Coupe (with a spoiler; did I mention the spoiler?!), I was the dude driving around at two in the afternoon with my headlights on so I could rock out.

• • •

Why does it seem like our lives aren't working when we need them to work?

Why do we lack the power to live the way we want?

Why do we often make so many irrational and self-defeating decisions?

Why do we try so hard to change but end up doing the things we hate?

We have crossed wires.

You've seen it in yourself, right? I mean, why do you

- ► commit to stop arguing with your sibling, then keep arguing with your sibling?
- ► worry nonstop even though you know it's a waste of time and makes you sick?
- ► exaggerate to impress others even though that's not the kind of person you want to be?

> ▶ scroll on your phone for hours instead of talking to your family members, who are sitting only a few feet away?

You have crossed wires. We all do.

The reason we make these poor decisions is because of how our brains work. So we need a solution that works with the way we think. We have to not only recognize the unhealthy patterns but also figure out the underlying problem. Stop the car, crawl under the dash, and find out what went wrong.

If we want to win the war in our minds, we have to be willing to rewire our thought patterns—rewire our brains.

> If we want to win the war in our minds, we have to be willing to rewire our thought patterns—rewire our brains.

Stuck in a Rut

In Alaska, there are only two seasons: winter and July. When the weather gets warm in the summer, the snow melts and the dirt roads become muddy. Cars drive on them, creating long ruts. There is a sign along one Alaskan road that reads, "Choose your rut carefully. You'll be in it for the next sixty miles."

You probably know what being in a rut feels like. Thinking the same thoughts, doing the same things, experiencing the same problems. It's like we're hopelessly entrenched on a muddy, rugged back road.

And when a rut gets really deep, when your tires are all the way inside, you can let go of the steering wheel and the vehicle will just keep going down the road. Stuck in one direction with no options to get out or get off until the rut ends.

So let's talk about how our brains work.

Every thought you have produces a neurochemical change in your mind. Your brain literally redesigns itself around that thought.

The brain is a command center that directs the parts of your body through neurons. Neurons link together to create messages. The same message sent multiple times will create a neural pathway. The presence of a neural pathway makes a thought easier to think and makes it easier for your body to send that same message again.

Think of neural pathways as ruts in your brain.

Now, how do ruts get created? Let me tell you about a cute little mini collie named Bandit that I once owned.

Oh, Bandit's color, you ask? C'mon, what color dog do you think someone with my unbridled coolness would have? Brown. Yes, my dog was the same color as my 1979 Buick Century (upgraded with the spoiler, eagle decals, and nighttime-only stereo—the car, not my dog).

Bandit had a big yard to run around in but for some reason always ran in a circle in the exact same path. That pattern killed all the grass on his repeated, precise route and eventually created a circular rut that made it look like an alien spaceship had landed in our yard.

In a similar way, repeated thoughts create paths in our brains. Again, neural pathways are brain ruts.

These ruts are often carved deeper by the bundle of nerves at the base of our brain stem known as the reticular activating system (RAS). The RAS sifts through millions of pieces of sensory data being sent to our brains and groups them according to relevance and similarity. If the information will keep us alive, prevent problems, avert danger, or bring pleasure, the RAS is activated. It's your brain's system for filtering through all the data in your life and allowing you to focus on what's most relevant and ignore the rest.

Our RASs also utilize our established beliefs to screen incoming information. This is part of the reason we so often get what we expect. It's called "confirmation bias," a term coined by Peter Wason, a cognitive psychologist at University College, London. Confirmation bias is looking for and liking information that supports things we already believe or value—which can include interpreting any new information according to those beliefs. It's the definition of being stuck in a mental rut because it is easier than seeing things from a different perspective.

What Is Bias?

The word *bias* came down through Old French and means something like "a slant or slope," but the way we use this term today actually comes from an old lawn game like bocce ball called "bowls."[3]

In the game of bowls, the balls aren't perfectly round, and are weighted on one side. When rolled, these balls don't roll straight. Skilled bowlers can factor in the natural bias of these balls to get nearest to their goals.

We all have some natural biases that cause us to roll toward some things and away from others. When we recognize our biases, we can account for them and still get near our intended goals, but when we pretend we are without them, we'll be continually frustrated when we can't get things to roll straight.

If you keep thinking you're a victim who never gets a chance to succeed or that no one loves you, you are training your brain to look for evidence that supports that belief and to filter out evidence that doesn't. You condition your brain to reinforce what you already believe. You create a victim rut. The tires drop in, you let go of the steering wheel, and you travel down the victim road.

And because your brain is designed to look for patterns and create neurological pathways, they help you keep thinking the things you keep thinking and doing the things you keep doing.

This is also why thinking new thoughts or trying new things is awkward the first time. Remember when you first tried to ride a bike or play the piano or do long division? You thought you would never get it. But as you do that thing again and again, it becomes effortless. (Except for maybe long division. But you know what I mean.) The saying "Practice makes perfect" makes even more sense now, doesn't it?

Creating and reinforcing new neurological pathways— new ruts—is hard work, but here's a tip to make it easier: sleep on it.

Sleep isn't just something you do during math class or boring sermons. Scientists think sleep might be the key to consolidating memories and learning into our brains. That's why staying up all night to cram for a test is a bad idea. If you want to actually remember what you've studied, you'll study right before bed, then get eight or nine hours of sleep.

How does it all work? Imagine learning as taking notes with a pencil during class. The things that are important to know, you trace over again and again until the pencil line is

Teen Sleep Facts

- While babies and children tend to wake early and get to sleep early, teen brains are wired to stay up late and sleep in late. This is related to the fact that melatonin, a hormone that helps us sleep, is released in teens two hours later than in children or adults.
- If given the opportunity, teens would sleep between nine and ten hours per night. (Sound like you at all?)
- Some research suggests that teens who use their cell phones after "lights out" get less sleep than they otherwise would, plus they're more likely to suffer from mental health disorders.

Adapted from *The Teenage Brain: A Neuroscientist's Survival Guide to Raising Adolescents and Young Adults* by Frances E. Jensen, MD, with Amy Ellis Nutt (Harper: 2015).

dark. But you doodle while you learn too. By the end of the class, your notes are covered in doodles and you realize it's not as useful a study tool as you were hoping. So what do you do? You erase what you can. Soon, your doodles are gone, replaced with little bits of eraser, but the notes you traced over and over are still there and much easier to see.

Sleep is the eraser that takes away the unimportant information. Repetition of thoughts will lay down the neural pathways. Getting enough sleep will keep those pathways clear, making it easier to reinforce them.

Okay, sleep habits aside, all repetition of thoughts—good

or bad—creates and reinforces the formation of neural path-ways. Thinking or doing something again and again eventually becomes effortless.

God created neural pathways to be a good thing. When we repeat helpful thoughts and practices, they create helpful ruts that keep us moving in healthy ways. But because of our sin, neural pathways can also be a bad thing. Why? The same reason you felt awkward the first time you

- ► saw someone naked pop up on a screen.
- ► thought of yourself as a victim who can never win.
- ► responded to a bad experience by going shopping and spending way too much money.
- ► passed along some juicy but hurtful gossip about a good friend.

Feeling uncomfortable, you thought, *This is dumb. Why am I doing this?* You may have felt guilty. But you also got a little jolt of pleasure. That buzz is a chemical your brain releases called dopamine. That little natural high is your brain's way of saying, *I like that. Let's think that again! Let's do that again!*

How Does Dopamine Work?

Dopamine is both a hormone and a neuro-transmitter. That means it does a couple differ-ent things in your body. When it works as a hormone, it triggers certain changes in your body. When it works as a neurotransmitter, it sends those buzzy messages to the reward circuits of your brain.

Basically, when you do something your brain thinks will help it survive, it wants to encourage you to do it again, so it releases some dopamine. The more dopamine that gets released along that neural path, or brain rut, the more reward circuits your body makes to feel those pleasurable reward messages.

For example, when you eat junk food, your brain says, "These extra calories will help us not die if we can't find food tomorrow," and it makes more dopamine for you as well as more connections to get more dopamine. The result is that you get more pleasure when you eat junk food and you'll crave junk food more often, which can easily lead to addiction.

The main challenge for you as a teenager is that while your body is making all these dopamine-charged choices about reinforcing what feels good, the wires linked up to the part of your brain that helps you think through whether a choice is good or bad isn't fully wired yet, so it takes longer to make rational choices. Sadly, by the time the part of your brain that thinks things through gets its message out there, you've already made a decision based on your dopamine receptors.

Because of your body's craving for those hits of dopamine, you escaped into the glow of a cell phone, snuck some alcohol from your parents' stash, or lied to a friend to get out of something. This time felt a little less awkward, and you got another hit of dopamine. That led you to do it again. The third time was much easier. Why? You were developing a neural pathway.

Do the same thing enough, and you will have a rut that you fall into automatically.

You were designed to smoothly, efficiently create and fall into habits, into neurological ruts.

That is helpful for brushing your teeth.

That is harmful for rating your self-worth by constantly referring to social media.

If you find yourself stuck in unhealthy, unproductive ruts, there's some good news: God has given us a way out.

Recognizing the Rut

In part 1, we worked on identifying the lies we believe. We agreed that lies can be hard to detect, so it helps to identify the problems that plague us.

As you think about what you think about, you might notice some common harmful thought patterns. I know I do. We are wise to recognize these mental ruts we repeatedly travel that knock us off the path we know God wants us to be on.

One of my most frustrating mental ruts involves finances. I am always tempted to believe the lie that I can find security in money instead of in God. Hey, just being real. In my heart, I know and believe that God is my provider. Yet my thoughts get trapped in the same old rut of worrying that I won't have enough to provide security and stability for the people I love.

So I identified a lie I believe that leads me into an irrational, self-defeating mental rut. What should I do next? You know from the previous chapter: ask probing questions.

Why do I believe this lie? When did this false belief start? My grandmother (who is in heaven now) is one of my heroes. I respected her so much, and her words meant every-thing to me. When I was little, Grandma and I loved to sit on her front porch and watch the cars pass in front of her house.

She loved to tell me stories, often ones I'd heard before, about the funny things my mom did when she was a little girl. I would eat a cherry-flavored popsicle and laugh like I was hearing them all for the very first time. The conversation was always light and playful. Until one day when it wasn't.

I'm not sure why she chose that day to tell me about her childhood during the Great Depression. Although I did not fully understand her thinking back then, I clearly understand the effect it has had on my thinking to this day.

I sat on Grandma's lap as she shifted from storyteller to teacher. She did her best to explain to me what sparked the Great Depression. Then she started shaking as she recalled the horrors that she, like so many others in her generation, had suffered through. She cried as she described people eating out of garbage cans to survive and those who had lost hope and jumped out of windows. Grandma looked me in the eyes and warned, "Craig, I love you so much. You need to know that the economy *will* fall apart again in your lifetime. And when it does, you need to be ready."

That idea was new and confusing, but I believed my grandma. I started worrying about money, dreading the day when I wouldn't have enough. So if someone gave me cash for my birthday, I would hide it under my rug. The slow-growing little lump in my bedroom floor represented where I was put-ting my hope. Someday the economy would crash, but I would be able to buy food for my family. I was doing exactly what Grandma had warned me to do.

You might think that as I got older, I would be able to think about money more clearly. Nope. My brain had already formed neural pathways. Every time I thought about money, my reflex reaction was to worry and try to create financial security.

I worked hard to pay off any and every debt. Just five years into our marriage, Amy and I had paid off all of our debt, including the mortgage on our small house. Being debt free puts you in a strong financial position that should lead to freedom. Not for me. Money and security were still a constant source of anxiety. I still made irrational decisions. Even ordering what I wanted at a restaurant was difficult for me. If cheese cost extra, I wouldn't add it to my burger. Pretty stupid, right? Could I afford the extra fifty cents? Of course, but it was almost impossible for me to think that way.

My mindset was driven by a deep fear of not having enough, even while I didn't owe anyone and I made plenty of money. Why? I had spent years developing neural pathways, and the easiest thing was for me to fall into those same unhealthy mental ruts.

Okay, it's your turn. What's your rut?

Maybe when you were younger, your mom's answer for every problem was food. When you were a baby, she gave you a bottle when you cried. When you were a toddler, if you fell down and skinned your knee, the solution wasn't a bandage but ice cream.

What does this lead to?

Your brain created a neural pathway. Neurons linked together, over and over, with the same message: if you are hurt or angry or sad, eat something; comfort yourself with food. Now eating is your built-in response to a problem.

Perhaps on the first day of first grade, you were picked last on the playground for kickball. You tried to make sense of that strange new feeling. What did it mean?

Then your father didn't treat you fairly, which felt familiar, a lot like what happened at recess.

All through middle school, your sibling was more popular than you, so you thought, perhaps subconsciously, *Huh, this is kind of like what happened on the playground and with Dad.*

Then your parents told you they were getting a divorce. *What? No! Why is this happening to me? My friends' parents aren't divorced. Bad things like this are always happening to me! It's like I'm cursed.*

What happened to you?

Your brain created a neural pathway. You began weaving these random, different, yet somehow similar experiences into a story you told yourself. You started to believe a lie that you are a victim. You can't win. People will always hurt you. Now, almost no matter what happens, your habitual response is to think that someone's out to get you and something is about to go wrong.

Maybe one night, you finished your homework and got bored. You started mindlessly surfing the internet, and then it happened. One click at a time, you wandered onto a site that showed seductive photos of a barely clothed body.

You felt awkward and guilty but also excited. You hit a dopamine jackpot.

The next time you were bored, the thought hit you: *I could try to find that website.* You did, and it was a little less awkward with a little less guilt.

A couple of days later you were bored again, and you quickly decided to find that same website. Actually, why not see what else is out there? You found new sites with nudity, and this time it all felt more intuitive.

Pretty soon you were making excuses to get alone in your bedroom, because all day you were thinking about finding more websites and seeing more stimulating images and videos.

What happened to you?

Your brain created a neural pathway. God's original intention for you to have a pure mind was violated, and you began thinking thoughts you were never intended to think.

A Wake-Up Call

In all these examples, including my own, wires got crossed. Normal life events occurred, fair or not, intentional or not, and we turned the opportunity into a bad connection that formed an unhealthy pattern that created a toxic rut. In the case of my grandma's advice, I could still have made the healthy decision to be wise with my money and live debt free while being inspired by her stories to be generous to the down-and-out and be grateful for all my blessings.

And Bandit, my brown dog? Well, he stayed on that same path with that same pattern for all of his dog years. But you have an opportunity adults don't have. Due to brain plasticity (more on that later), you are better able to change your ruts and thought patterns right now than at any other time in your life.

Know this: Unless we decide to break the unhealthy patterns, our lives will continue moving in the wrong direction. In a circle that never goes anywhere. It's normal. Easy. The same old rut.

But I'm guessing you want something different, something better.

EXERCISE 4

recognizing *your ruts*

In this exercise, I want you to write down any places in your life where lies have crossed your wires and created ruts in your thinking. Using what you wrote in exercise 3 and considering the many examples I gave you in this chapter, ask God to speak to you and reveal the origin of your ruts. If at all possible, as in the situation with my grandma, try to go back to the source.

Whether or not you can discover where these things began, the primary goal of this exercise is to write down and face any and every harmful, hurtful rut that has been created in your mind. You are walking through a personal journey, one step at a time, that can lead you to a renewed mind and a changed life.

My ruts:

part 2: the rewire principle

creating a trench of truth

A while back I made a solemn vow that I would stop obsessing over texts and social media. I decided that any time I heard the *bing* indicating I had received a message, I would not feel the urgency to check immediately. And when I did check, I would not reread and reread what the other person wrote. I would then not rewrite and rewrite my response.

My digital resolution didn't last long. Social media addiction is a real thing!

Can you relate?

 A recent study in JAMA Pediatrics says screen time outside of virtual school among kids twelve to thirteen doubled from pre-pandemic estimates of 3.8 hours per day to 7.7 hours.* (See? I'm not as alone in my unhealthy screen time habits as I thought.)

Another study from Common Sense Media found

that teens and tweens increased their media usage by 17 percent between 2019 and 2021**—a bigger increase in two years than researchers saw over the previous four.

---

*: https://jamanetwork.com/journals/jamapediatrics/fullarticle/2785686

**: https://www.commonsensemedia.org/sites/default/files/research/report/8-18-census-integrated-report-final-web_0.pdf

The problem with how we attack our problems is that we go after the problem. We focus solely on the behavior by making a commitment to start or stop doing something.

You know what I mean, right? You've decided, perhaps even declared, that you were going to change.

- ► I'm going to go to bed earlier so I can get some sleep before my alarm goes off!
- ► I'm going to stop letting other people's opinions of me change who I am!
- ► I'm tired of wasting my time on social media and comparing my life with everyone else's. I'm getting off for good this time!
- ► I'm going to watch my words and not listen to any more music with language I know isn't helpful.
- ► That's it. This is the last time. I will never look at pornography again!
- ► I'm not going to exaggerate or lie or gossip to get attention or feel better about myself. No more!
- ► I'm going to show up for youth group each week and read my Bible or devotional every day.

Whatever your vow was, how did it go?

I would guess not well. Why? Behavior modification doesn't work, because the focus is only on modifying behavior. You don't get to the root of the problem, which is the thought that produces the behavior. To be more specific, the problem is the neural pathway that leads to the behavior.

Let's say you just finished an hour-long bike ride on the hottest day of the year after neglecting to put on deodorant. Your eyes burn as sweat drips from your saturated eyebrows. Your shirt clings to you like plastic wrap on hot leftovers. And the smell . . . It's like a skunk who's been eating red onions curled up and died in your armpits.

Face it. You're tipping toward the unpleasant-to-be-around side of the scale.

So you wash your hands and head off to hang out with your friends.

Only, when you get there, your friends plug their noses and send you away.

How could this be?! You washed your hands! What is their problem?!

I know. The analogy is absurd. If you smelled as bad as what I described, you'd need a long shower and some powerful bodywash (lather, rinse, repeat at least five times). The problem can't be fixed by simply washing your hands. It goes a lot deeper than that. If you don't get down to the source of the stink, you aren't going to smell any more pleasant. And no amount of body spray is going to cover the problem.

Well, if we decide, *I'm going to stop spending every minute staring at a screen* or *I'm going to stop isolating myself and living a lonely life* or *I'm going to exercise every day*, we're just washing our hands and hoping for the best. We are ignoring the real problem of the lie we believe and the mental rut we fall into. Attacking only the surface, not the source.

Thinking I can change a behavior just by removing the behavior is absurd. The behavior isn't the deeper problem. The neural pathway that leads me to the behavior is the problem. If I stop a behavior, it will come back, unless I

1. remove the lie at the root of the behavior, and
2. replace the neural pathway that leads me to the behavior.

Throughout part 1, we learned how to remove the lie and replace it with truth. Now let's discover how we can create a new neural pathway, or to put it another way, dig a new and helpful trench. This is going to help us rewire our brains and renew our minds.

To make sure we understand what we're talking about, let's spell out the differences between our two similar words:

A *rut* is typically formed in mud and becomes a nuisance, even a danger. A rut is unintentionally created, has no purpose, and requires repair.

A *trench* is intentionally dug to deliver a necessary resource. A trench has a specific purpose and fixes an existing problem.

We know that the only antidote for a lie is truth. That's why our first tool was the Replacement Principle: Remove the lies, replace with truth. The antidote for a negative neural pathway is a new neural pathway. Instead of living in a rut, you can create a truth trench that runs deeper, diverting the flow of your thoughts from old pathways to new ones.

We have a series of set thoughts we think each time we are triggered. For you, the trigger might be feeling alone, fearing failure, or being around people who are making bad choices; you fall into the same series of thoughts you always fall into, and they lead to the same behavior. We are now going to strategically choose a new series of thoughts.

Where will we get these new thoughts? Hint: we won't get them from scrolling through the same social media posts, listening to our favorite playlist, or from friends who are struggling with the exact same issues.

To stop the lies and replace them with truth, we need to look to God's Word.

To stop the lies and replace them with truth, we need to look to God's Word.

Remember, that's the weapon God gives us for the battle we are fighting. His truth is what can set us free, and we are going to choose specific Bible verses to create a new neural pathway that applies directly to our problem. Using his Word, we will create a trench of truth.

For this to work, we need to do more than just know God's Word; we need to internalize it. The author of Psalm 119 understood this when he wrote, "I have hidden your word in my heart that I might not sin against you" (v. 11).

That's what Jesus did. He had verses memorized that applied directly to temptations he faced. When Satan tempted him, Jesus couldn't whip out his iPhone and open up the YouVersion Bible app to search for a verse that might help. (To be completely honest, he could have because he's Jesus, but he didn't because he didn't need to.) He had already internalized truths from God's Word that created a helpful neural pathway. When tempted, Jesus followed that path, leading him to obedience and freedom.

That's what we need to do.

So let's see how another tool can empower us to overcome the unhelpful and unhealthy patterns that have held us hostage and are keeping us from the life God intends for us to live.

Determining Declarations

The second tool for changing your thinking is the Rewire Principle: Rewire your brain, renew your mind. I told you earlier about my financial rut. Any trigger about money leads me to fear, thoughts of how I don't have enough, and my need to save more to create security. When I am triggered about money, I fall into a rut—that's the way my brain works—so I need to create a trench of truth.

The good news is that the Bible speaks to all our problems. God's Word gives us truth that empowers us to break out of the old ruts of destruction and onto a new path that leads to life. What does the Bible say that applies directly to my fears and issues about money? Here are some of my verses:

> ▶ "I know what it is to be in need, and I know what it is to have plenty. I have learned the secret of being content in any and every situation, whether well fed or hungry, whether living in plenty or in want" (Philippians 4:12).

- ▸ "It is more blessed to give than to receive" (Acts 20:35).
- ▸ "God will meet all your needs according to the riches of his glory in Christ Jesus" (Philippians 4:19).

From these I put together what I call a "declaration"— what I am declaring to be true in my battle against the lies I am tempted to believe. The goal of the declaration is to have it become my new neural pathway, my intentionally dug trench of truth.

Here's my declaration based on God's Word:

Money is not and never will be a problem for me.
My God is an abundant provider
who meets every need.
Because I am blessed, I will always be a blessing.
I will lead the way with irrational generosity,
because I know it's truly more
blessed to give than to receive.

That's just one of my declarations that speaks directly to a problem that has plagued me for years.

What new neural pathway do you need to create? That depends on your old pathway, right?

Let's go back to some of our past examples.

In your old rut, maybe you saw yourself as a loser. You've wrongly believed that people are constantly looking down on you, that they think you aren't cool or worthy of their time. That has not led you into the life you want, so you create a trench of truth using verses you find in Romans 8. Your declaration could be:

God is for me, so who can be against me?
My God is working all things for my good.
I am more than a conqueror through Jesus,
who loves me and gives me strength.

Maybe you struggle with lust. As a teen, it'd be a miracle if you didn't. Your brain is wired to release tons of dopamine when you see a bit of skin. When you're online, at the beach, or anywhere, your eyes and thoughts go places you know they shouldn't. So you create a declaration, based on truths found in God's Word, that becomes your new neural pathway, your trench of truth:

Lust is not my master.
God has redeemed me and
given me pure thoughts.
I will not look lustfully,
because I've made that covenant with my
eyes and with my God, who strengthens me.
God is always faithful and, when I am
tempted, will always provide a way out.

Draw your declarations from God's truth and make them your own. Be creative. Write your declarations in a way that will speak to and inspire you. Put them in places where you can quickly see them and memorize them. Put them in the notes on your phone so you can immediately swipe away and scroll to them. Repetition will dig your new trench deeper and deeper, making the new pathway easier and more accessible. Write your declaration as if it were already true, even if you don't fully believe it yet. With a new declaration, we are claiming the victory we have in Christ, and we need to create a neural pathway that affirms our ability to demolish the stronghold and win the battle.

All this might feel silly at first. Remember, anything new can feel strange in the beginning. You will be saying something you want to believe, but your life will be saying something different. That's okay. Don't be discouraged. Don't give up. The gravitational pull toward your old negative thoughts will likely be stronger than you can imagine. Resist those lies. Keep renewing your mind with God's truth, and it will become true of you.

Write It, Think It, Confess It

For years, I thought that if I went to the gym, threw some weights around, and grunted a lot, I would somehow be in good physical shape. What I didn't realize was that even more than what I do *with* my body, physical fitness is about what I put *in* my body. If I am to be truly healthy, what goes into me has to be healthy.

The same is true with our minds. What we put in our minds comes out in our lives. Every action we take, every word we say, and every attitude we express originates in our thoughts.

But what's crazy is how little attention we give to what goes into our minds. People who have high performance cars put in only high-octane gasoline. People who care about

> What we put in our minds comes out in our lives.

their dogs choose pet food that has antioxidants and the right balance of meats, vegetables, grains, and fruits. We can be so careful about what we put into our cars or feed our pets yet so careless about what we put into our minds.

One reason we need to be extra attentive about these decisions is because we constantly have thoughts we did not choose. Studies reveal that we are bombarded by about five hundred unintentional and intrusive thoughts a day.[1] Each unwanted thought lasts about fourteen seconds. Do the math. That's almost two hours a day of thoughts we do not want to think.

Two hours of thought missiles like, *You aren't good enough. You deserve better. If they knew you, they wouldn't like you. You will always be alone.* If we don't do something, those thoughts will poison our thinking. We really do need to win the war in our minds!

Psychologists and others who study how our minds work talk about the law of exposure. The law of exposure says that the mind absorbs and reflects what it is exposed to the most. Basically, if we allow a thought into our minds, it will come out in our lives.

More than two thousand years ago, our thoughtology teacher Paul taught us that same truth when he wrote, "Those who are dominated by the sinful nature think about sinful things, but those who are controlled by the Holy Spirit think about things that please the Spirit. So letting your sinful nature control your mind leads to death. But letting the Spirit control your mind leads to life and peace" (Romans 8:5–6 NLT).

Paul taught that if you allow a thought into your mind, it will come out in your life. So if you want to change your life,

you have to change your thinking. You need a new declaration.

We need to be intentional
about what we allow into our
minds! Why? Because what consumes our minds controls our lives.

> If you want to change your life, you have to change your thinking.

That's why I meditate on truth, specifically on Bible verses
that apply to my strongholds and on the declarations I have
written to create new neural pathways.

Now, I don't know what springs to mind for you when
you encounter the word *meditation*, but I can tell you what
the biblical understanding of it is: focusing one's thoughts on
the things of God. The Bible talks *a lot* about meditating.
We are told to focus on, to meditate on, God's goodness and
God's Word.

Eastern meditation is an emptying of your mind. What
I'm suggesting—what the Bible calls for—is the opposite.
Christian meditation is filling your mind with God's truth,
being strategic and deliberate about what you allow into your
mind. We make the law of exposure work for us instead of
against us. We win the war in our minds by creating a solution
for our mental ruts: trenches of truth that work with the way
our brains work.

We'll talk more about meditation in the next chapter, but
for now I want to encourage you to meditate on the truths that
apply to your problem. Here's the plan: write it, think it, and
confess it until you believe it.

EXERCISE 5

digging

trenches of truth

In this chapter, we dug even deeper into what it means to meditate on God's Word and then convert biblical principles into lifelong declarations. I want to give you another opportunity to pray and ask God for trenches of truth and declarations to remove the lies you've been believing. Focus on your own life. Dig your trenches of truth deep, allowing God to renew your mind and transform your life. Remember:

Write it. Think it. Confess it. Until you believe it.

Lie:

Truth:

Declaration:

Lie:

Truth:

Declaration:

rumination and *renewal*

Are you ready for some fun facts about cows? It'll make sense in a few minutes, I promise

- ▶ Cows can see in almost panoramic vision. Because their eyes are positioned on the sides of their heads, they can watch for predators from every direction.
- ▶ Cows can smell things from six miles away. So by the time you smell a cow, it's probably already smelled you.
- ▶ Cows don't have upper front teeth. They do have sharp bottom teeth that cut grass by pressing against the hard palate on the top of their mouths.
- ▶ Cows will chew about forty to fifty times per minute for up to eight hours a day.
- ▶ Cows are ruminants, or cud-chewing animals. There are around two hundred species of ruminants out there, but here are a few whose names begin with G: gazelles, giraffes, and goats.

▸ The main stomach of a cow, the rumen, holds up to fifty
gallons of partially digested food. (The average bathtub
holds between thirty and fifty gallons of water.)[1]

*Okay, that's neat (and gross), but what does it have to do with
winning the war in my mind?*

Good question. In Joshua 1:8, Psalm 1:2, and at least six
other passages in the Psalms, God tells us to ruminate. The
word *meditate* in these verses is the same as the word *ruminate*. What does ruminate mean? Well, as we learned, cows
are ruminants (cud-chewers) and their main stomach is called
the rumen. Rumination is how cows digest their food.

Cows get a mouthful of grass, chew it up (with only those
bottom teeth and a hard top palate), swallow it, throw it back up
into their mouths, chew it some more, swallow it again, throw it
back up into their mouths, chew it some more, swallow it again,
throw it back up again, chew it more, swallow it again. They do
this over and over and over. That is what it means to ruminate.

That is the exact idea behind the word meditate.
Meditating is taking a thought—in our case a Bible verse or
a declaration based on God's Word—and chewing on it, then
swallowing it, then bringing it back to mind and chewing on
it some more. Then we swallow it again, then bring it back
to mind and chew on it more. We do that over and over and
over. We aren't talking about casual Bible reading; we mean
repeatedly taking in every word, the meaning, and the context.

Why? Well, why do cows ruminate on their cud? Because
it allows them to get the maximum amount of nutrition out
of the grass.

Why do we meditate on God's truth and God's love and

God's great deeds? One reason is because it allows us to get the maximum amount of spiritual nutrition out of our godly thoughts.

There's another reason: repetition is the reason for ruts.

When you envision my dog Bandit running around the yard, or people driving on a muddy road in Alaska, it's obvious that one time does not a rut make. The reason for a physical rut is repetition.

The same is true for our mental ruts. Want to hear something fascinating? Increasingly, research proves that the way to get someone to believe a lie is to simply repeat the lie.[2] Psychologists call this the "illusory truth effect." When something is repeated over and over and over, we're more likely to believe it is true.

Repetition is the reason for ruts.

This is why our spiritual enemy whispers the same lies to us repeatedly. He knows that the more often we think a thought, the more likely we are to believe it, and the more likely it is for the lie to become a rut we get stuck in.

Have you noticed that the devil keeps whispering the same lies to you? He is just being repetitive, not creative. If he were creative, today he'd tempt you to fight with your parents, and tomorrow with your mail carrier. But my guess is that it's always your parents, and you might not even know who delivers your mail. If Satan were creative, today he'd tell you you're not pretty enough, and tomorrow that you don't perspire enough. But I bet you've never feared that you lack the ability to sweat.

So how will you overcome his repetitive lies? How will you replace the old rut with a new pathway? The answer is repetition.

> Write it, think it, confess it until you believe it.

You are going to write the truth, think it, and confess it until you believe it.

Speaking your declarations once will not really do anything. You have been told lies over and over, and you now need to tell yourself the truth over and over. Meditate, chew, ruminate, swallow, repeat. As the self-help author Napoleon Hill said, "Any idea, plan, or purpose may be placed in the mind through repetition of thought." Repetition is what creates the rut, but it is also what will create the new trench.

Write it, think it, confess it until you believe it.

Do this as early as possible each morning. What we are thinking about now influences what we think about next. So what you think about first thing in the morning is the first domino to fall, impacting your thoughts for the rest of the day.

What does that mean?

You should start your day in God's Word, digging trenches of truth and finding your declarations. Then write it, think it, confess it until you believe it.

Of Centipede Dilemmas and Godly Autopilot

Have you ever done something without thinking about it?

It might be hard for you to imagine if you're just starting to drive, but drivers who have followed the same route for years fall into a kind of "highway hypnosis" and arrive at their destination only to wonder how they got there. Quite possibly unsafe, but it happens all the time.

Or if driving isn't your thing yet, hopefully hygiene is.

When you take a shower, you don't wonder, *What part of me should I wash first? How do I wash my hair? There are so many things to think about.* No, you get in the shower and do everything you need to do without thinking. While one part of your brain is taking care of cleaning you up, another part is thinking about the day to come or the day you just had.

These things are possible because of *automaticity.* Automaticity is the ability to do things without thinking about what you are doing because past repetition allows an action to become unconscious, automatic.

And guess what! You're using automaticity right now, just by reading this book. When you read, you're actually doing a bunch of things automatically at the same time. Your brain is decoding the words, figuring out what they mean, relating them to concepts and information you already know, guessing at how they might apply, and deciding whether the stuff they are talking about is useful. The more you read, the faster this process gets. This is why it takes kids who are just starting to read a long time to digest the information, but it hasn't taken you long at all.

Automaticity.

But automaticity isn't all magical experiences and shower shortcuts. It has a dark side too. Some scientists suggest that prejudice and stereotypes are a kind of automatic thinking. And if you've already learned some unhelpful habits, automaticity will keep you doing things you don't want to do. Repetition has led to negative, harmful things becoming automatic.

We need to break the automatic responses in the harmful areas and lean into automaticity for the good ones. The answer in both situations involves some conscious thought.

> *The Centipede's Dilemma*, as it was published in the
> scientific journal *Nature* on May 23, 1889:
>
> A centipede was happy—quite!
> Until a toad in fun
> Said, "Pray, which leg moves after which?"
> This raised her doubts to such a pitch,
> She fell exhausted in the ditch
> Not knowing how to run.

There's an old psychological term known as "the Centipede's Dilemma" based on an anonymous poem from the 1800s. In the poem, a centipede is stopped in its tracks when a toad asks how it walks. The truth it illustrates is that when we try to think about something we've been doing automatically, we suddenly find that we can't do it.

That's helpful when we are trying to disrupt our unhealthy thoughts. Now let's focus on using automaticity to reinforce good ones.

The goal of meditating on God's Word and on our declarations is automaticity. We want to create a new trench to lead us into the right thoughts and actions. Automatically. An old quote states, "Watch your thoughts, they become your words; watch your words, they become your actions; watch your actions, they become your habits; watch your habits, they become your character; watch your character, it becomes your destiny." The journey to your destiny starts with your thoughts. The right thoughts lead to the right life. Automatically.

learning to *ruminate*

Today's exercise is straightforward: choose a verse or passage, possibly one you found for a truth in exercise 5, and practice ruminating—chewing it over and over, swallowing, bringing it up again, then repeating this process—and meditating as I taught you in this chapter.

A few helpful suggestions for this process are:

1. Look intently at each word and phrase, one at a time. Don't make any assumptions or skip a single word. Each one is important to the overall meaning for you.

2. Type your Scripture reference into your search engine and look for online Bible commentaries. Read what some of the great Bible thinkers—aka *theologians*—have said about the meanings of the Hebrew or Greek words used in your verse or passage. This level of personal study can bring new meaning as you apply the truth in your life.

3. Ask God, the author of the Word, to speak to your heart about anything specific he might want to say to you through your verse or passage.

My verse or passage:

the reframe principle

*Reframe Your Mind,
Restore Your Perspective*

Trust in the Lord with all your heart,
   and do not lean on your own understanding.
In all your ways acknowledge him,
   and he will make straight your paths.

—Proverbs 3:5–6 ESV

lenses and *filters*

Imagine a friend drives you to a party. Just before you both walk into the house, your friend grabs you, looks you in the eye, and says, "Remember that embarrassing thing you told me over text? Well, my phone got hacked and there's a good chance everyone in there is going to know about it. Oh well, let's party!" You're shocked. A cold wave of panic travels through your body and you can't seem to breathe right, but your friend is already through the door. You walk in behind them because they are your ride home.

Everything at the party would look different to you.

If you see two people whispering and laughing, you know what they're talking about—you and your embarrassing secret!

If you try to make eye contact with someone but they seem preoccupied with their phone, you can tell they are reading the hacked text.

Finally, when your friend is ready to leave, they say, "You know I was just kidding about getting hacked, right?" You give him a confused look. He smirks and lights up. "I wouldn't tell anyone your secrets. Gotcha!"

No one actually knew anything embarrassing about you, but because you assumed they did, you looked at everything through that lens. Remember, a lie believed as truth will affect your life as if it were true. We could say a lens with a distorted view will make lies seem like they're true.

I wonder how often you see what you expect instead of what's really there—reality the way reality really is.

I'm Not Biased. You're Biased!

Social psychologists have a name for our distorted lenses. They call it a cognitive bias. Remember earlier when we learned about confirmation bias—the tendency to look for and like information that supports things we already believe or value? Well, a cognitive bias refers to our tendency to believe something is real even if it isn't. It is when we process experiences based on a lie (like when your friend says everyone knows your embarrassing secret) instead of the truth (no one except that one friend knows your embarrassing secret). If you have a cognitive bias, you create a subjective reality. That construction of your reality, not actual reality, will dictate how you respond and behave in the world.[1]

That's a kind of scholarly way of thinking about cognitive bias, but you don't need that explanation. You see people with a cognitive bias all the time.

You might have a teacher who writes the same feedback on a research paper in the same way to two students. One receives it as fair, constructive criticism. "That really helped me see a flaw in how I wrote my paper. I appreciate the feed-back. This will improve how I write papers in the future."

The other person is totally offended. "How can she say that about my work? Who does she think she is? You want some feedback? I'll give you some feedback!"

What is the difference? Cognitive bias.

Perhaps the second person has a demanding, insulting parent and now sees every authority figure through that lens.

Studies show that cognitive bias changes how a person sees God. Your relationship with your earthly father often influences how you see your heavenly Father. If you have a good dad who is involved and full of compassion, it's easier to view God as relational and caring about the details of your life. If you have a father who is absent or abusive, you are more likely to think of God as distant and disinterested. Same God. Different filter.

You can recognize cognitive bias in others, but can you in yourself?

Part of the problem is that we don't tend to see our own cognitive biases. Because if we knew it was a bias, we wouldn't have one.

That's why it's so important to think about what you think about. You cannot defeat an enemy you cannot define. Ask probing questions to explore why you think what you think.

> That's why it's so important to think about what you think about. You cannot defeat an enemy you cannot define.

As I've practiced these disciplines over the past few years, I've discovered my cognitive bias toward believing I'm not enough and needing to prove myself. And toward thinking I don't have enough and need to get more to provide financial security.

What about you? How does your cognitive bias block your path to progress? More importantly, what are you going to do about it?

Let's work to define our cognitive biases so we can defeat them.

Control Freak

Hi, my name is Craig and I am a control freak.

That's not a cognitive bias; that's just a fact. When I say I'm controlling, I mean that I am *controlling*.

Get in a car with me and see who's driving. I am. Does not matter who else is in the car or whose car it is. I'm driving. Yes, I will drive you in your car. And if for some end-of-times, sign-of-the-apocalypse reason someone else is driving the car, there is a good chance I will grab the steering wheel from my seat and take over. You think I'm kidding? I'm not kidding. Because I'm controlling.

Are there some ways in which you're controlling? How would your family or friends answer that for you? Perhaps you use reverse psychology on your parents, drop not-so-subtle hints to your friends about your expectations for the weekend, or humblebrag to your teacher to make sure you get personal credit for the group project they assigned. Those are all control issues.

Here's the problem: being in control is an illusion.

I don't like to admit this, but I cannot control what has happened to me, and I cannot control what will happen to me.

Neither can you. No matter how hard you try, you cannot control what's happened in the past or what will happen in the future. That's bad news, but there is good news.

You cannot control what's happened or what will happen, but you can control how you perceive it.

Social psychologists have a name for taking control of how we perceive things. They call it cognitive reframing.[2] It's when we learn to identify and correct irrational thinking. We could say this happens when we un-bias our bias.

Our frame is how we view things. It's the cognitive bias we use to understand what's happening in our lives. Reframing is when we decide we are not going to hang on to old perceptions that have worked against us. We are going to choose a different, more godly, more productive way of thinking.

Experts in the psychotherapeutic world share steps that help us to reframe, to take control of our thoughts and overcome our cognitive bias, such as:

▶ *Stay calm.* If you react, you will probably react the way you've always reacted.
▶ *Identify the situation.* What exactly, and truly, is happening?
▶ *Identify your automatic thoughts.* If I trip over someone's foot as I'm walking up the steps to my school, my automatic response is to panic and assume everyone is laughing at me. I can't control someone's foot tripping me up, but I can control how I perceive it. So instead of thinking my automatic thought, I identify that thought. I can take it captive and make it obedient to Christ. Then I take an additional step:

▶ *Find objective supportive evidence.* I want to deal with reality, so I search for objective data on which to base my thinking, such as: People trip. It happens to everyone. No one has a right to laugh at someone tripping. There is no reason to freak out.

> You cannot control what happens to you, but you *can* control how you frame it.

You can take these same steps. You cannot control what happens to you, but you *can* control how you frame it.

And who in the Bible was the master of reframing? That's right! It was our thoughtology teacher, the apostle Paul.

Paul had a plan for spreading the gospel—go to Rome. If he could get to Rome and preach Jesus to the leaders there, the city could become a launchpad to spread the gospel all over the world.

The Roman empire was in full swing at the time. Things that happened in Rome influenced what happened in a huge chunk of the world. It's estimated that during this time, every one in four people on earth lived and died under Roman rule. Paul believed that if he could spread the gospel in Rome, Christianity could spread along the Roman roads throughout the world.

And Paul *did* get to Rome, but it wasn't to share Jesus with government officials. He went there as a prisoner. He was locked up under house arrest, chained to a rotating group of guards, awaiting a possible execution. Paul prayed for an opportunity, but it was not happening.

Paul's circumstances were out of his control. Circumstances are almost always out of our control.

You've been where Paul was.

You thought, *If I just get this accomplishment, I will get that boyfriend or girlfriend.* You accomplished the thing, but you did not get the relationship.

You've been praying for your home life to change, but God has not answered that prayer.

Paul was in that same situation—circumstances he did not want and could not control. He wrote to the church at Philippi about what was happening to him. What might he have said? He could have written, "Now, I want you to know, brothers and sisters, that what has happened to me really stinks. I wanted to spread the good news through preaching to government officials, but that did not happen. As a result of this hell I've been through, I have decided prayer doesn't work, and I am never going back to church again."

But that is not what Paul wrote. Could have been, but no. Remember, Paul couldn't control what happened to him, but he could control how he framed it. Here's what he actually wrote to the Philippians: "I want you to know, my dear brothers and sisters, that everything that has happened to me here has helped to spread the Good News. For everyone here, including the whole palace guard, knows that I am in chains because of Christ. And because of my imprisonment, most of the believers here have gained confidence and boldly speak God's message without fear" (Philippians 1:12–14 NLT).

Paul was saying, "I had a plan, but God had a better plan! This is a whole different way to advance the gospel than what I was thinking. God has blessed me with prison guards who are chained to me. They have no choice but to listen to me tell them about Jesus! These soldiers have the ear of influential leaders! And, get this, every eight hours they chain a new guard to me! And they think I'm the prisoner. Ha! God is moving. I can't wait to see what he does next!"

You cannot control what happens to you, but you can control how you frame it.

The third tool to change your thinking is the Reframe Principle: Reframe your mind, restore your perspective. (The first tool is the Replacement Principle: Remove the lies, replace with truth. The second tool is the Rewire Principle: Rewire your brain, renew your mind.) Reframing has changed my thinking and changed my life.

Reframing your past—and preframing your future—will change your life.

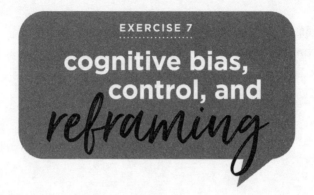

cognitive bias, control, and *reframing*

Cognitive bias can be difficult for any of us to identify in our own lives. But looking for these areas and becoming aware of our thoughts and beliefs to this degree can help us win the war in our minds.

In this exercise, write down any biases or places of control you may have thought of as you read the chapter. Consider talking with a parent, loved one, or friend and asking them to help you identify some of the biases and control issues they may see in you. You aren't inviting criticism; you're looking for the opportunity to remove blind spots and grow. Finally, pray, think, and write down any potential ways you can reframe your biases or areas of control.

My cognitive biases:

Areas of control regarding people, places, or circumstances:

Ways I can reframe biases and control issues:

what God didn't do

Back when I was in middle school, the DJ at the roller-skating rink would crank songs by the J. Geils Band. A huge sing along-while-you-skate J. Geils hit was "Freeze Frame." The song featured such Shakespearean-level lyrics as "It's like the freeze, she's breeze." Don't judge. Song lyrics haven't gotten more sophisticated over time. Anyway, "Freeze Frame" was about savoring a moment so much that you want to stay in it forever.

There are special moments in life we would love to stay in forever.

There are also sad moments in life we can get stuck in forever. They are not the moments we want to freeze-frame, but too often we do. Those formative moments can become the lens through which we view what happens for the rest of our lives. They form our cognitive bias, the frame we use to define our reality.

You may not have as much of a past as the grown-ups

around you, but you've still got a past, right? There are things you get stuck on. Stuff you wish you could go back and do over. Mistakes you've made. Frames you get stuck in. What better time than when you are young to get unstuck from these unhealthy versions of reality?

We need to unfreeze our frames. We need to go back and rewrite the narrative we have been telling ourselves.

> We need to unfreeze our frames. We need to go back and rewrite the narrative we have been telling ourselves.

So how do we reframe our past?

We thank God for what he didn't do.

We look for God's goodness.

This is the shortest chapter in the book, but it might be one of the most powerful. Here's why: it will reframe your past. Thanking God for what he's done is easy for most of us. But I've learned to also thank God for what he *didn't* do.

To discover those blessings can take a long time, but when you finally have that aha moment—wow! Here's an example from my life.

My dad played professional baseball. I was born and bred to be a professional baseball player. Most infants are given milk and Cheerios. I was given Gatorade and sunflower seeds.

I grew up believing that my dad expected me to follow in his footsteps, to carry our family name into the Baseball Hall of Fame in ways he didn't have the chance to do. And with good baseball genes and great baseball coaching, I seemed to have a real future in pro ball. Until the accident.

I was in eighth grade. My baseball team was the best in

our league. We made it to the championship, and our coach told me I would be the starting pitcher in the big game.

Let's review: Professional baseball dad. Family expectations. Championship game on the line. No pressure, right?

The night before the big game, we went to a batting cage. Normally, I would hit in the one that was appropriate for my age. This night I was feeling like a big-timer. I decided to go to the batting cage with the fastest pitch, meant for college-level players and semipro wannabes. But I was sure I was ready. Just think about how proud my dad would be when I crushed the ball at college levels as an eighth grader!

The first pitch was inside and, before I could get out of the way, crushed my pitching hand against the bat. My fingers were broken, shattered into pieces.

Needless to say, I did not pitch the next day. I could not play for a long time.

Because of how I was raised, baseball was everything to me, so I felt like my life had been shattered as badly as my hand. I could not understand how God could let something like this happen to me. Inside, I was in a rage.

Then our family moved to another city. Let's be honest, moving stinks. Losing your friends and having to make new ones is not fun. Not only did we move; we moved to Ardmore, Oklahoma. Want to know what Ardmore is known for? If you are driving from Dallas, Texas, to Oklahoma City, Ardmore is where you stop to go to the bathroom. That's right. We moved to the pit stop town.

When we moved to Ardmore, it was not baseball season. It was tennis season. *Tennis? No thanks.* I knew nothing about tennis. I was not interested in playing tennis.

Except . . . there was a cute girl on the tennis team. So, tennis? *Sure, I'll play tennis.*

The tennis player was a normal, cute Oklahoma girl. Since I did not yet have an awesome Buick with a spoiler, I would have to impress her with my tennis playing ability. Except I had never played tennis. Still, I tried out and, amazingly, I made the team.

Six people qualified to compete on the traveling team. I was number six, the last guy to make the team. When baseball season came around, my plan was to drop tennis and go back to the sport I loved. But the thought of having pitches coming at me brought back memories of having my fingers broken. So I decided that taking a year off would be good for me. I stuck with tennis, and we placed second in the state that year.

The next season, a few guys graduated and I had improved, so I somehow ended up winning the number one spot on the team. That year we won the state championship. I kept playing tennis through the rest of high school.

After graduation, I received a full-ride tennis scholarship to a college I never would have gone to otherwise. That college is where I fell deep into sin and where I met Jesus in a life-changing way. A lot of people started making fun of me for being a Jesus freak. One day a girl said, "You are so weird for Jesus. There's a girl at another school who's weird for Jesus like you. Her name is Amy. You two should meet and get married."

That is exactly what happened. Boom!

And why did that happen?

Because of what God *didn't* do. He didn't answer my prayer to protect me and prepare me for the championship baseball game. Because of what God didn't do, I got a full scholarship in tennis, a sport I never planned on playing, at a college I never planned on going to, where I met Jesus and my wife!

Think about some of the things you've wanted and prayers you've prayed. It may be difficult to see without the benefit of more time, but I bet you've got things to be thankful for. Things that God didn't do, even if you hoped he would at the time.

Think about some of the worst circumstances you've had to go through. You never would have chosen them, and maybe you prayed God would pull you out of them, but didn't they help you grow in ways that are crucial to who you are today?

Think about some of the best parts of your life right now. Aren't some of them things you never imagined or planned for, but wouldn't have happened without the Father making them happen?

Sometimes we need to thank God for what he didn't do. Developing that discipline helps us reframe our experiences.

Why? Here's why: "'My thoughts are not your thoughts, neither are your ways my ways,' declares the Lord. 'As the heavens are higher than the earth, so are my ways higher than your ways and my thoughts than your thoughts'" (Isaiah 55:8–9).

> Sometimes we need to thank God for what he didn't do. Developing that discipline helps us reframe our experiences.

We are wise when we trust that he is working even when we aren't aware of it. We are also wise when we trust the way he's working, even when it isn't the way we want. Because instead of feeling like a victim of random circumstances in a chaotic world, you see you have a God who has protected you, often from yourself, in ways you didn't realize.

It only makes sense: If God knows more than we do (and he does), then certainly there will be times when we ask for things he knows are not good for us. In his goodness, then, he says no to those requests. The problem is that we never think we're asking for something that isn't good for us. I knew that I needed to play baseball in high school. And God was gracious enough to say no.

Now when I think about stepping into that batting cage, I have a perspective that's different from the one I had a week after my bones shattered. What happened that day remains the same, but the meaning has been changed by the reframe.

EXERCISE 8

unanswered prayers

Think back through your life on your past hopes, dreams, desires, and relationships. Think through some what-ifs in a positive, good way. See if you can come up with situations from your life, much like the personal example I gave you, in which God didn't answer your prayer or allow your dreams to come true. See these situations through the filter that he knew all along what was best for you. This can be an amazing and eye-opening glimpse into the deep love your heavenly Father has for you.

God, in my life, I thank you that you didn't:

9

collateral *goodness*

Have you heard the term "collateral damage"? It refers to the bad things that happen during a military offensive, specifically to people who are uninvolved with the conflict. It can take years for the public to find out about the unintentional effects of a war, because at the time it happened, the focus was on the battle at hand.

The word *collateral* means to happen alongside something else. Just like there is collateral damage, there's collateral goodness too. For the war that's waging in our minds, we need to start searching for the good that happens alongside the bad. And while collateral damage isn't intentional on the part of the generals leading the war, God's collateral goodness in our lives happens for a reason.

Like any good habit, looking for God's collateral goodness requires practice.

Remember, *confirmation bias* is the tendency to look for and like information that supports things we already believe

121

or value. When you already believe the world to be a bad place where bad things happen, that's all you are likely to notice. If you look for things to be critical of, there is always going to be something to criticize.

On the other hand, if you look for God's goodness, you will see it. You'll start seeing his fingerprints and occasionally feel like he's winking at you. As you pay attention to how God is working, you will also find yourself seeing the good in people. This practice will change your relationships.

> If you look for God's goodness, you will see it.

You might be familiar with the story about how Moses led the Israelites out of Egypt and Pharaoh's army chased them to the edge of the Red Sea. The Israelites were caught between death by drowning if they went forward and death by swords and trained warriors if they stayed put. Then God parted the sea and they escaped, miraculously walking along the seafloor, water piling up on either side of them.

There's an ancient Jewish story—a *midrash* or commentary on God's story—about two guys named Reuven and Shimon who were walking through the parted Red Sea: "As they walked through the sea, all they could talk about was the mud. Reuven said: 'In Egypt, we had mud, and now in the sea we have mud. In Egypt, we had clay for bricks, and here too, we have an abundance of clay to make bricks.' They rebelled at the sea, even though this was the parting of the [Red Sea]! They didn't notice the water, they only saw the mud."[1]

You find what you are looking for.

Unfortunately for me, and maybe for you too, looking for God's goodness has been a struggle. Negativity and lack of gratitude has been another stronghold in my life. Open up any social media app or listen to the day's news, and too many things in our world can feel hopeless. Even while God is miraculously making a way for me and the waters are piling up on either side of me, I'm throwing myself a pity party in the mud.

In my life, I have to consciously make an effort to continue looking for God's goodness and be grateful. Of course, change isn't immediate. But over time the reframe works! Searching for God's goodness has transformed my attitude. I've stopped feeling sorry for myself because of certain things and started feeling more satisfied, even amazed, at the life God has gifted me.

> We find what we are looking for, and we reframe by looking for God's goodness.

It's Friday, but Monday's Coming

After a busy weekend, do you ever feel wiped out when Monday rolls around? Going from sleeping in and not worrying about homework to early mornings in math class? I don't know about you, but on Mondays, I'm still mostly dead and just trying to recover.

Mondays are often dark days. My head hurts. I'm in a fog. I can't make wise decisions. You know what I'm talking about? I concluded a long time ago that I just have to endure Mondays. The valley of Mondays is the price I pay for mountaintop Saturdays and Sundays.

One particular Monday I was up early, doing my daily Bible study. Not because I wanted to but just because I'm supposed to. Like paying attention in early morning math class, but spiritual because I'm a pastor.

I read a verse that I had read at least a hundred times. But this was the first time I had read it on a Monday. Psalm 118:24: "This is the day that the LORD has made; let us rejoice and be glad in it" (ESV). Yet this time I didn't read the verse; the verse read me. I realized Mondays are from God. He made them. I did not have to frame every Monday as a bad day. I could "rejoice and be glad in it." After all, God made Mondays just as he had the other six days.

I decided to reframe my Mondays, starting that day. I started declaring this freshly applied truth from God's Word: "This is the day the Lord has made. I will rejoice. I will be glad in it. I will look for God's good hand. I will see his favor at work."

Guess what happened? That Monday was a better day. Not perfect, but better. Ever since, I have reframed Mondays by looking for God's goodness, and Mondays just keep getting better.

We find what we are looking for, and we reframe by looking for God's goodness.

Once again, I want to be real with you: this is not easy. Well, I can say it's not been easy for me. Sure, I make progress, but there is always something pulling me back to my old way of thinking. That's the nature of a stronghold; demolishing them takes divine power and continual mental discipline. And some fall far more slowly than others. I've often found that when I think I have victory and the battle is won, there's still battling left to do.

Do you need to reframe your past? Do you need to thank God for what he didn't do, and start looking for his goodness?

You could be set free. Free from being haunted by things you have done and things that were done to you. Free from mindsets that have kept you shackled to your past. Free from ruts of self-defeating habits.

Wouldn't you like to be free? You can. Reframe your life, and experience the blessings of God's collateral goodness.

Preframe Your Future

When we reframe what happened in our yesterdays, that changes our todays. We are able to experience life without the old, negative cognitive bias and start seeing through the lens of God's goodness.

Just as we can reframe, we can also preframe.

Preframing is choosing how I will view something before it happens. Instead of getting there and letting my old way of looking at things take over, I proactively choose the frame I will use to think about my experience.

> When we reframe what happened in our yesterdays, that changes our todays.

I first learned to preframe from my high school tennis coach, even if I didn't know what it was called then—look at how far ahead of me you are already! As I mentioned before, early in my tennis career I went to the state championship. Somehow I was in the quarterfinals, playing against Mandy Ochoa. He was a senior. I was a sophomore. He was a legend. I was a nobody. He was ranked fourth in the state. I was ranked nothing. Apparently, they didn't have enough numbers to rank someone like me.

But as we played, I had him against the ropes! We split sets. The crowd was getting hyped. You could hear them murmuring, "Who's this little kid about to dethrone Mandy Ochoa? Did you see the spoiler and eagles on his cool brown car? This unranked kid could win the state championship! He was cranking some sweet beats! But why did he have his headlights on in the middle of the afternoon?"

I had Ochoa down five games to one in the final set. The game count was 40–love. One more point and victory would be mine.

In the final set, I had seven match points. Match point means that if you win the point, you win the whole match. Seven times I had match points! Seven opportunities to knock off the number-four-ranked player in the state!

I lost all seven. I was up five games to one in the third set, and I lost seven to five.

I was nicknamed Craig Gro-choke-el. In Oklahoma, people started saying, "If the matches get tight, Craig will lose. He's Craig Gro-choke-el."

You may want to take note of that. It's pretty significant. The frame through which you look at the world may not be one you picked up on your own. Sometimes other people force the frame on you.

- ► Your father says you will never amount to anything.
- ► Your mother makes you feel unattractive and body conscious.
- ► Kids at school tell you to just accept the fact you are a loser.

▶ A grandparent insists only rich or educated people are
  important.

Maybe you have a cognitive bias built by other people. You
accepted what they told you as truth, and even though it was
a lie, it's affecting your life as if it were true.

When everyone in the Oklahoma tennis circuit started
saying, "Craig chokes in big matches," my coach decided to
put a stop to what he knew would only limit me. He looked
me in the eyes and said, "No! That is not true, Craig. Do not
own that label." He explained, "You now have more experience
that will help you succeed than anyone else. You have been in
that tight spot. You know what doesn't work. You know that
when people get nervous in sports, most start playing not to
lose. You need to play to win. Instead of not taking risks, you
need to push harder, swing harder. You will be better because
you lost. From now on, you will use your experience to rise to
the occasion and win."

From that day on I have told myself, *Groeschel, you are a
pressure player. You are at your best when things are at their worst.
In those moments, your God is for you and your God is with you.*

My declaration for tennis became one for pressure situations in life. In leadership, the tougher the circumstances,
the more I want to be involved. If there's a spiritual situation,
if someone is about to die who doesn't know Christ, let me
be the one to have the conversation. Why? I have preframed
the outcome. I will walk into it knowing my God is for me
and with me. I will not play to lose. I will play to win. I am a
pressure player. I rise to the occasion.

That's not just what I tell myself. That's how I live and handle those tough moments. Because I can't control what happens to me. But I can control how I frame it, how I think about it. And the way I frame it will dictate how I respond and behave.

This isn't just wishful thinking. I'm now telling you to "believe and achieve." I'm saying that your brain is hardwired to set you up on the path you mentally travel most often. Preframing your thoughts builds the network of connections in your brain needed in order to succeed. We're using the brain science God designed for every human being to do the things he has planned for us!

How do you need to preframe your future?

What situations do you know you will be walking into?

What would be the most positive, life-building, God-honoring, mutually edifying way for you to approach that moment?

Preframe it. With God's help, you can choose the frame through which you will step into that situation.

Let's say you wake up already feeling overwhelmed by the number of things you have to do—study for a science test, write a report on *Romeo and Juliet*, sports practice, and music lesson. Instead of complaining about how hard it will be, preframe it with a more positive, godly perspective. Tell yourself, *Today I get to experience God's strength when I am weak. He gives me everything I need to do what he's called me to do. Rather than a busy, bad day, I'm going to have a positive, productive one.*

If you are nervous about the challenging conversation you need to have with a friend, try to preframe it with faith.

Instead of imagining a blowup, thank God ahead of time for your friend and for giving you the words to say. Decide you are going to do the right thing and trust God with the results.

Know there's a different way to look at the world. We can choose to make our cognitive bias the goodness of God. We can look at our circumstances through the lens of his mercy and grace. There is not a moment when we have been forsaken or forgotten.

We can't control what happens to us, but we can control how we frame the outcome, even before it happens.

EXERCISE 9

your collateral
goodness

Think about your life. Has God ever allowed you to experience a difficult circumstance or relationship that turned out better because of how you preframed it? What happened to change your mindset?

Ask yourself, "In what relationship or circumstance do I struggle to see anything positive or good?" Write it out.

What is one practical step you could take to change your mind about this situation?

What would you want to see God do to change this situation?

What would be the most positive, life-building, God-honoring, mutually edifying way for you to approach this situation?

You can use this exercise to continue to reframe circumstances in your life and open doors for God to give you a new perspective. Remember, you can't control what happens to you, but you can control how you frame it. And the way you frame it will dictate how you respond and behave.

PART
4

the rejoice principle

Revive Your Soul, Reclaim Your Life

Praise the LORD.

Give thanks to the LORD, for he is good;
  his love endures forever.

—Psalm 106:1

problems, panic, and
presence

Blue vans, man. Blue vans freak me out. If one drives by, my heart beats fast and I'm ready to rush the driver or run for my life.

Why?

When I was a kid, my dad was driving our family home after dinner at our favorite hole-in-the-wall burger joint. Another driver who did not approve of my father's post–burger-fries-and-shake driving followed us to our house. We pulled into our driveway, and a blue van screeched in right behind us. Like a scene from an action movie.

A very angry guy got out of the van, screaming. He strung together a combination of four-letter words that would make a drunk fraternity boy blush. The man came running toward our car, nostrils flared, eyes wide, fists clenched, and lunged at my dad.

Bad decision. My dad can hold his own, and the man soon ran back to his blue van, in one piece only by the grace of God.

That night, my mom sat me down in the living room and explained in no uncertain terms that there was a man out there who was extremely angry with my father and probably our entire family. This man now knew where we lived, and he drove a blue van. She warned me, "If you ever see a blue van, run inside, lock the doors, and call the police."

My mom's loving yet stern warning felt much like my grandma's prophecy about another financial depression. So another pattern of fear emerged. For years, every time I saw a blue van, I would run inside, lock the doors, and hide under my bed. Just like Mom told me to do.

To this day, I go into high alert if I see a blue van. A blue van is a threat and pushes my panic button.

Teens and Stress

 What's going on in your brain when you face a stressful situation?

As soon as you detect a threat—like someone angrily approaching you, people laughing at you, or blue vans driving by—your limbic system jumps into action. The limbic system is the emotional center of the brain and includes the amygdala, hippocampus, hypothalamus, and a few other parts.

When you face a threat or experience any strong emotion, your amygdala messages your hypothalamus to start up your autonomic nervous system. This causes your heart rate to increase, your breathing to pick up, and your blood pressure to skyrocket. Your body is getting ready for action, either fighting or fleeing (or more unhelpfully, freezing perfectly still). Hormones are released into your bloodstream, and your brain takes in information faster than any other time. In fact, time feels like it slows down a bit.

What's different for teens is that some of the hormones that get released when you face a stressful situation act differently based on your stage of development. Researchers at the State University of New York reported in 2007 that tetrahydropregnanolone (THP) helps modulate anxiety in grown-ups but has the opposite effect in teens. This creates a feedback loop of stress in teens.[1]

Another difference between teens and adults is the developmental stage of the frontal lobes, the logical thinking part of the brain. In teens, this area isn't fully wired yet. When an adult faces a stressful situation, their body gets ready for action, but part of their brain sends a message to the frontal lobes and asks, "How should we respond to this threat? Is it even a threat?" But for teens, those messages can be easily lost on the route between the emotional and logical parts of the brain. This leaves the emotional area with more control over how teens react in stressful situations.

I bet you have some threats that lead you to panic. They may be a little irrational, like my aversion to blue vans. Or they may be very real.

What perceived threats cause you to panic? Not being able

to control your future? A bad grade? Someone giving you a funny look? A friend who takes their time replying to your text or doesn't respond at all? The thought that you might fail?

We've said your life will always move in the direction of your strongest thoughts. That's good news if you are thinking on things that are noble, right, pure, lovely, admirable, excellent, or praiseworthy. It's bad news if you are thinking on things that are dishonorable, false, ugly, anxious, unjust, fearful, or just plain irrational. Our runaway negative thoughts can spiral out of control and lead our lives in the wrong direction.

> Our runaway negative thoughts can spiral out of control and lead our lives in the wrong direction.

So why do we panic?

As discussed in Teens and Stress, you can blame the amygdala. God gave us that almond-shaped part of the brain to help us stay safe in the face of danger. The problem is that the amygdala is not objective. The way it responds to a hurtling cow tornado (I live in Oklahoma, where there's an average of one tornado per week and lots of farms) is the same way it responds to a hurtful conversation. The way it responds to a noise letting you know a burglar has broken into your house is the same way it responds to a notification letting you know your best friend is no longer your best friend.

If you are confronted with an angry bovine or an aggressive burglar, you need the adrenaline to spark your body into action. If you are facing a disappointing text, you do not need the adrenaline, and it will just loiter in your body, acting as an unwanted hype man. You will feel stressed, agitated, on edge. Can you spell P-A-N-I-C?

What makes you panic? How about I confess mine, and perhaps you'll feel comfortable admitting yours.

Manic Panic

Before I unpack what causes me to panic, I want you to know I am not bragging or complaining. I am also not saying my world is more difficult than anyone else's. Everyone has their own stuff, their own issues. My world is not more difficult, just different. You may wish you had my problems and vice versa.

I struggle with what I call content anxiety. A big part of what I do is creating content. With sermons for my church, speeches at conferences, quarterly messages for our staff, episodes for my leadership podcast, and multiple weekly video leadership trainings, I can be working on a dozen messages at once.

Maybe you understand this. There's a good chance you have some kind of social media account. Even if you know spending time staring at a screen and rating your self-worth by whether people like your online persona is a dangerous hobby, you probably understand the stress of trying to make quality posts that will engage your friends and followers.

For me, not all messages—sermons, podcasts, and so on—take equal effort. I can prepare some of the smaller ones relatively quickly. But the bigger ones take from twelve to sixteen hours per message. Occasionally, they will demand up to twenty hours.

Working on twelve messages for at least twelve hours per message is, well, a *lot* of hours. I often feel like there are simply not enough hours available to do all the work I need to do. So to try to manufacture more hours, I started to wake up earlier and stay awake later. I'd often get up as early as three thirty in the morning to study, go all day, and then work after the kids had gone to bed at night.

Contrary to cultural belief, pastors do more than just preach on Sunday. I also have to fit in meetings, train new employees, give pastoral care, and so forth. The demands for my time go on and on. As a teen with schoolwork and extracurricular activities and friend stuff and family responsibilities, you understand the demands of time as well.

Yet my stress is not just about hours and workload. I don't just have to write messages; they have to be creative and relevant—all of them. And here's the reality: Every time I read the Bible, nothing in it has changed. The world is created. Adam and Eve sin. The earth floods and the ark floats. The bush burns and the sea parts. Every Christmas, the Virgin Mary has a baby, and his name is Jesus. Every Easter, the tomb is empty.

Don't get me wrong: These truths changed my life. I am honored and humbled to preach the good news every week. I just feel a constant pressure to present the Word in a way that will continue to impact people's lives. Tell the same stories with a new framing. Customize to the ever-changing culture without ever compromising the message.

In the summer of 2019, for the first time in my ministry, I hit a wall. I had no new ideas, no insights into Scripture, no revelation from God, and nothing meaningful to say.

I was empty. I felt scared beyond description. I had to fight to catch my breath. It seemed like the walls were slowly closing in around me. For the first time in more than a quarter of a century as a pastor, I wondered if maybe I had pushed too hard, had nothing left to give, and should just hang it up. Fear gripped me. Panic set in. Life became a massive, confusing, heart-wrenching ball of uncontrollable anxiety.

What was happening? My amygdala went into overdrive, doing double duty, sending adrenaline in a stampede through my body, leaving me in a panic like I had never experienced before.

All right, there is my honest confession. (Did you get a little tense just reading about the way I felt?)

Does my confession make you feel better? Maybe things aren't as bad as you thought! Or you might wonder why you're reading a book on winning the war in your mind by someone so messed up. Either way, I was honest. Now it's your turn.

What about you? Be gut-level honest. What makes you panic?

Believe it or not, simply being able to identify your stressors by name can help you get control over your stress response. Neuroscience tells us that it takes about ninety seconds for the chemicals that trigger your fight-flight-or-freeze response to get into and out of your bloodstream.[2] This means it'll take about ninety seconds for your brain to consider rational thought, and any response after that is your body hanging on to the emotion it caused. Which means that noticing your body's reaction to stress early can help you pull out of the stress earlier too.

Because God designed the stress response, it is by no means a bad thing. In fact, the stress itself can point us in helpful directions when we stop to think about what it is telling us. It can be helpful to write down the things you know

141

One of the best things you can do when you are stressed is pray. One, because prayer and meditation have been shown to help shift our thinking away from the sources of our stress. And two, because God can answer our prayers and use our situations for his glory. More on this in the next chapter!

stress you out and what that stress is telling you in order for you to change your thoughts and behaviors when you feel stressed.

Not in the Wind but in the Whisper

What causes us to panic?

For me, it's the presence of problems. Typically, it's not just one problem. We start getting into *I'm losing it and I really need a hug* territory when it's problems—plural. Multiple problems. You start feeling like you're playing whack-a-mole. You can handle *an* issue, but when they keep coming, you get to a point where you've had enough. That's when we need to master our minds, fix our thoughts, and worship our God.

Elijah had had enough.

He was a prophet who confronted the evil King Ahab about his sin and prophesied an impending drought. Infuriated, King Ahab threatened to kill Elijah, but the prophet managed to elude his hunter and eventually even confronted 850 false prophets, finally emerging victorious.

With such an incredible triumph, Elijah must have thought that was the end of his problems. But it wasn't. Evil

King Ahab had an even more evil wife named Jezebel. She was evil on steroids.

Jezebel decided, *If you want something done right, let a woman do it. My hubby couldn't get rid of Elijah. I'll kill him.*

Elijah realized that even after his great victory, his life was still in danger. He couldn't believe it. It was too much. Elijah was spent. His runaway negative thoughts spiraled out of control and led him into a deep depression. He prayed he would die.

Notice how irrational that is. His biggest fear was that Jezebel would kill him, so . . . he wanted to die. It doesn't make sense. But Elijah was not thinking clearly. Because he was at the end of his rope. He had hit the wall.

Done. Finished. Broken. Over it. All of it.

Have you been there? Reached the place where you cannot handle one more thing?

That's where Elijah was. "'I have had enough, LORD,' he said. 'Take my life, for I am no better than my ancestors who have already died'" (1 Kings 19:4 NLT). Notice how he's allowing his negative thoughts to run away and control him. From *I've had enough* to *I'm no better than my ancestors* to *They're lucky because they're already dead.*

I can do the same thing. Can you? From *My life is so hard* to *I can never get it all done* to *I don't like my life* to *No one understands* to *I can't stand all the pressure* to *It's always going to be like this.*

Why? Because of problems. We get fixated on the presence of our problems, and we lose our focus on the presence of God.

God was with Elijah every step of the way, with faithful, visible power and often miraculous provision. Yet when Elijah faced problems, he forgot God.

Elijah's name should have been an ever-present reminder of his ever-present God. The *El* in Elijah is short for *Elohim*, which means God. The *I* means "my." *Jah* is a way Israelites shortened *Yahweh*. Yahweh (or Jehovah) is the name of God. Elijah's name meant "Yahweh is my God," yet ironically he felt God was absent from his life.

> We get fixated on the presence of our problems, and we lose our focus on the presence of God.

Remember the words Paul wrote from prison? "Rejoice in the Lord always. I will say it again: Rejoice! Let your gentleness be evident to all. *The Lord is near.* Do not be anxious about anything, but in every situation, by prayer and petition, with thanksgiving, present your requests to God. And the peace of God, which transcends all understanding, will guard your hearts and your minds in Christ Jesus" (Philippians 4:4–7, emphasis added).

In the middle of trying to help people understand how they can rejoice and experience peace, Paul wrote, "The Lord is near." Recognizing God's presence will give you peace when you have cause for panic.

Elijah forgot the Lord was near. He needed a reminder. God gave him one—he revealed himself. "The Lord said, 'Go out and stand on the mountain in the presence of the Lord, for the Lord is about to pass by.' Then a great and powerful wind tore the mountains apart and shattered the rocks before the Lord, but the Lord was not in the wind. After the wind there was an earthquake, but the Lord was not in the earthquake. After the earthquake came a fire, but the Lord was not in the fire. And after the fire came a gentle whisper" (1 Kings 19:11–12).

God was not in the wind. God was not in the earthquake. God was not in the fire. Silence, then a whisper. God was in the whisper.

But why would God whisper to Elijah?

When you are overwhelmed and feeling anxious, if you listen for his voice, you'll find that God is whispering to you.

But why? Why does our God whisper?

He whispers because he is so close.

And he whispers to draw us close.

Think about it: When you are sitting next to a loved one and they whisper in your ear, what do you do? You lean into them. And you listen closely.

When we're hurting, when we're afraid, when we're overwhelmed, we may shout up to the heavens and wait for God to shout back. We wish for an audible voice. We don't understand why God doesn't speak loudly to us, commanding our attention in some obvious way. But why doesn't he do this? Why don't you hear him? Perhaps God wants you to slow down, to be still, to listen carefully for his soft, comforting, quiet voice.

Because you have to get quiet and listen intently. God whispers because he is close and because he desires to draw you close. Lean in and listen.

What did Elijah learn on the mountain that day?

When you've had enough, God is enough.

Elijah had endured so much hardship. He cried out to God, "I've had enough. I want to die!" Elijah didn't understand what he really needed. He didn't need to die. He didn't even need to have God solve all his problems. He just needed God.

When you've had enough, God is enough.

Experiencing God's Presence

Maybe you've been where Elijah was. You wouldn't be alone.

Let me tell you about a teenage friend of mine named Dave (not his real name). Dave was a lot like me, an overachiever. He was the youngest guy in his graduating class, got into a good school with some scholarships, and took as many courses as he could at one time (because college courses get more expensive every year you attend).

He had relationships with girls, but never healthy ones. He tried to do the right things so people would think he was a good guy. He joined a campus ministry and sang in the worship band, all the while taking almost twice the number of classes that would be considered a full-time load. It was all going well, until it wasn't.

While Dave did his best to hold together his good-guy image, he was dealing with a serious pornography addiction. He felt fake, and dirty, and tired.

Dave started thinking that maybe it would be easier if he wasn't around anymore. He saw his relationships through a broken lens and believed nothing could improve. He wanted it all to be over. Like Elijah, he cried to God, "I've had enough. I want to die!"

Let's be clear about this: Suicide is never going to improve things, but that doesn't mean people don't consider it. According to the National Alliance on Mental Illness, nearly 20 percent of high school students seriously consider suicide and 9 percent have attempted it. This has led to suicide being the second-leading cause of death among people 15 to 24.[3]

If you have thoughts like Elijah or my friend Dave—and

statistically speaking, at least one in five people reading this book do—there's help. Depression happens, but talking to someone is always, always, always better than acting on it.

Listen.

Just when Dave hit rock bottom, something incredible happened. He opened his eyes and realized the view from the bottom means there's nowhere to go but up. Dave's parents got him into counseling. He started taking medication to help him think more clearly. He realized his dependance on sin was holding him back from the life he wanted, the life God wanted for him. Step-by-step, Dave understood he wasn't the center of the universe.

When Dave tried to make himself happy—with the public approval of others and a private life of sin—he grew more and more miserable. But when he recognized God is the center of universe, he grew more and more content.

God spoke to Dave in the whisper, even as he wanted to end it all. Have you been there? Are you there now? God is there too. Just as he was with Dave, and Elijah, and me.

Back to 2019: I was experiencing the biggest breakdown of my life. My world came crashing down, and my life came to a screeching halt. My body shut down. It just stopped. Although I didn't go to the hospital, I did call a counselor. I knew I needed professional help. Counselors are great people.

Yes, I am a pastor, and yes, I am in counseling. As I mentioned earlier, there's no shame in that. Getting help isn't a sign of weakness. It's a sign of wisdom. Sometimes we need to talk through our stuff with someone trained in talking through stuff. Someone who has no agenda except to help us get well.

I started meeting with a performance psychologist who

helped me remember things I knew but had been ignoring. I recognized how faithful God has always been in providing spiritual content for me to preach. I had a long track record of experience, and there was no reason to think he was going to stop now. Even more, my psychologist pointed me to the Lord. Staring at my stressors was obscuring my view of my Savior.

Even if everything is entirely wrong, I still have a God who is entirely righteous. Even if I were left with nothing, I still have God and he is everything. When I was at rock bottom, I could finally look up and see God.

> What's getting in the way of your view of God today?

But I had to figure out how to stop fixating on the presence of my problems and refocus on the presence of God. I had to once again lean in close to hear God's whisper.

I already knew what I discovered in counseling, but still it felt like a surprise ending. I had the aha moment I needed. I created a new declaration. Remember, in order for truth to set us free, we need to internalize it. It needs to live inside us so it becomes an automatic response. How do you replace an old rut with a new trench? Repetition.

The new, liberating declaration I tell myself again and again:

God's presence is enough.

It's what Elijah learned. The experience he already had—with God providing miraculously for him, sustaining him through the worst of times—plus God's presence was enough.

It's what Dave learned. Life wasn't about how great he looked from the outside or making himself happy. He was most content when he focused on God's presence more than his own.

The same is true for you. You might be feeling burdened, overwhelmed, and anxious. Maybe your soul feels crushed. What you need is the surprise ending you've known all along.

When you've had enough, God is enough.

Yes, the presence of problems is tempting you to panic. But don't ignore the presence of God. God is bigger than you and bigger than your problems. The most essential thing for your mind is for your mind to stay mindful about the presence of God.

> When you've had enough, God is enough.

Declare these next statements in your life, for your life. Say them out loud.

> The Lord is close.
> He is near.
> He will never leave me nor forsake me.
> Nothing can separate me from his love.
> He is always with me. (He's with me
> right now as I read this book.)
> I am never alone, and he is enough for me.
> His strength sustains me.
> He watches over me, and he guides
> me with his loving eye upon me.
> God is close, and he wants to draw me close.
> I will lean into him and listen for his whisper.

The LORD is righteous in all his ways
    and faithful in all he does.
The LORD is near to all who call on him,
    to all who call on him in truth.
He fulfills the desires of those who fear him;
    he hears their cry and saves them.

—PSALM 145:17–19

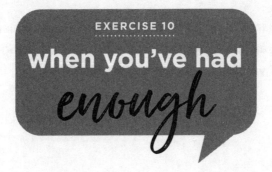

when you've had *enough*

What's happening in your life right now that regularly creates panic for you?

Why do you think these specific situations create panic in you?

Is there any place in your life right now where you would say you have had enough and are at the end of your rope? Write it out.

What can you do to lean in and hear God's whisper among all the wind, fire, and earthquakes going on around you now in this circumstance?

Would talking to a counselor, pastor, or close friend help you get to a better place with this issue? If so, who?

Go back to the end of the chapter and read out loud the declaration statement I gave you. God is near. He is listening.

the perspective
of *praise*

Why is being mindful of God's presence so critical?

What I'm about to tell you may seem stupidly simple, but it's indescribably important. Are you ready? Don't miss this.

If you forget God is there, you won't talk to him.

Simple, right? (I warned you.) But it's true. When we don't focus on God's presence, we don't pray. Instead, we go it alone. We find our thoughts moving in the wrong direction, and our lives quickly follow.

But when we realize God is there, we realize we can talk to him. When things are bad, instead of just feeling down, we look up. We look up and find a God who loves us and has the power to help. We need to practice God's presence—habitually reminding ourselves that God is with us—so we'll be persistent in prayer.

Remember Paul's prescription in Philippians 4 for panic-inducing circumstances? "Do not be anxious about anything, but in every situation, by prayer and petition, with thanksgiving, present your requests to God" (v. 6).

Let this game-changing truth sink in:

► If it's big enough to worry about, then it's big enough to pray about.
► If it's on your mind, then it's on God's heart.

So pray.

If you are starting to experience some runaway negative thoughts—you're worried about an upcoming doctor's appointment, you don't know what decision to make, you are concerned about how you're doing in school, your parents or caregivers aren't talking to each other—pray.

Something I've learned from years of being a pastor is that a lot of people aren't sure how to pray.

► Do I address God as my omnipotent Creator?
► Is praying in Old English with "thees and thous" required?
► Do I have to sign off with the whole "In Jesus's name" part?
► Is the word *harken* required? I hope not, because I'm not sure I know what harken means.

Well, harken to this: the answer to these is a no.

In the garden of Gethsemane before his arrest, Jesus called God *Abba*, the Aramaic word for *father*. Abba was the most simple, endearing way to refer to a father back then. Our equivalent might be *Daddy* or *Papa*. God is a relational God who loves you and wants to have an intimate relationship with you. You can call him Abba Father, the way Jesus did.

Paul wrote, "Present your requests to God," which may sound a little formal, but it's not. Another way of translating Paul's words is, "Let your needs be known." When you've had enough and your problems are tempting you to panic, how should you pray? Just let your needs be known.

You might talk your prayers, yell your prayers, sing or journal them. You might pray long or you might pray short; just make sure you pray. There is no perfect way. Just pray.

When you pray, ask with confidence. God is your perfect heavenly Father, and he loves it when you come to him and let your needs be known.

Peter told us that God invites us to go to him. "Humble yourselves, therefore, under God's mighty hand, that he may lift you up in due time. Cast all your anxiety on him because he cares for you" (1 Peter 5:6–7).

Do you feel down? Wiped out? Like you've had enough? Do you feel like you're sinking? Peter said, "Humble yourselves . . . under God's mighty hand, that he may lift you up."

Those words will be more meaningful if you think about who wrote them. Peter is the one who was in the boat with the other disciples and had the audacity to believe he could get out and walk on water to Jesus. He was taking step after step on the Sea of Galilee, probably walking like a toddler at a trampoline park, when he noticed the wind and waves. His thoughts started to run, spiraling into negativity. He became fixated on the crashing waves and howling wind. The presence of problems caused him to ignore the presence of Jesus. So he sank.

Peter was drowning, so what did he do? He reached out to find Jesus's hand. Jesus lifted him up and saved him. Years later, Peter had not forgotten, and he encouraged anyone who would read his letter, "Humble yourselves, therefore, under God's mighty hand, that he may lift you up."

This Is Your Brain on Prayer

Prayer works. Prayer changes things. Perhaps more important, prayer changes *you*. Prayer changes your brain.

Let's revisit the term neuroplasticity—the ability for our brains to change and adapt. Your teenage brain has more flexibility right now than at almost any other time in your life. Neuroplasticity is the idea that we can sculpt our brain just as we can sculpt our muscles with some strategic time spent at the gym. Your brain is rewiring itself all the time by creating those new neural pathways.

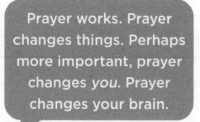

Each time you think a thought, it's easier to think that thought again. That's good news if you're thinking godly thoughts. It's not good news if you've been conditioned to run from blue vans.

Your brain is changing, and prayer changes your brain.

Dr. Andrew Newberg is neuroscientist and a professor and director of research at Thomas Jefferson University and Hospital in Pennsylvania. He studies the brain by using neuro-imaging techniques including functional magnetic resonance imaging, single-photon emission computed tomography, and positron emission tomography. I will shoot straight with you: I don't know what any of that means. But I do understand Dr. Newberg's conclusion. He writes, in scholarly articles and in books like *How God Changes Your Brain*, that prayer is like a physical workout for the brain and changes its chemistry.

Think about that. Not only does prayer touch the heart of God, but prayer changes the chemistry of your brain!

Another author in this field called neurotheology is Dr. Caroline Leaf, author of *Switch On Your Brain*. Her website says, "Dr. Caroline Leaf is a communication pathologist and cognitive neuroscientist with a Masters and PhD in Communication Pathology and a BSc in Logopaedics, specializing in cognitive and metacognitive neuropsychology."[1] I'm going to shoot straight with you again: I also don't know what any of that means!

Dr. Leaf writes, "It has been found that twelve minutes of daily focused prayer over an eight-week period can change the brain to such an extent that it can be measured on a brain scan. This type of prayer increases activity in brain areas associated with social interaction, compassion, and sensitivity to others. It also increases frontal lobe activity as focus and intentionality increase."[2]

At this stage in your life, your frontal lobe is still getting wired up. That means two things: Remembering to pray might be more difficult when you are just starting out with this process. And there's no better time than right now to start wiring the prayer-minded connections into your frontal lobe.

Your life is always moving in the direction of your strongest thoughts. Worrying and toxic thinking will change your brain and move your life in a direction you don't want to go. Prayer changes your brain and moves your life in a positive direction.

Remember what Paul wrote? "Do not conform to the pattern of this world, but be transformed by the renewing of your mind" (Romans 12:2).

From conforming to being transformed and renewed. Prayer literally renews our mind, leading us to God's peace and understanding. "And the peace of God, which transcends all understanding, will guard your hearts and your minds in Christ Jesus" (Philippians 4:7).

So why do we panic? It's that obnoxious amygdala. Scientists have a name for what happens to us, first coined by Daniel Goleman in his book *Emotional Intelligence*: an amygdala hijack. The amygdala gets a peek at what's going on out there and has an immediate, emotional, and overwhelming response, often a disproportionately excessive reaction. *Blue van! Run! Now!*

How do you avoid becoming a hostage to your amygdala? How do you counter its negative impact and not allow it to bully you into a panic?

You pray.

I know, I get it, that sounds like something pastors are supposed to say, but we can find peace through prayer! We can control our brains through prayer! It *is* something pastors say but also something scientists say. Another one of Dr. Andrew Newberg's findings startled the scientific community. He discovered that prayer can regulate and decrease the amygdala's fight-or-flight response.[3]

A scientist would call what happens to us when we panic,

worry, and freak out an amygdala hijack. Paul, coming from a spiritual perspective, described this as sinful thinking. What is that?

Sinful thinking is not trusting the promises and power of God.

Prayer is choosing to trust the promises and power of God.

Prayer is deciding to turn to God and surrender our feelings and control of our lives to him, trusting his promises and power. That's what we're going to do. We are going to pray in faith.

Paul wrote, "Those who are dominated by the sinful nature think about sinful things, but those who are controlled by the Holy Spirit think about things that please the Spirit. So letting your sinful nature control your mind leads to death. But letting the Spirit control your mind leads to life and peace" (Romans 8:5–6 NLT).

If we let our natural, human nature take over, we will be led by runaway negative thoughts that spiral out of control and lead us in the wrong direction. If we let the Spirit take over, we will be led to life and peace.

This is why it is critical we take every thought captive. With the power of the Holy Spirit, we are going to prayerfully start building up our prefrontal cortex as a burly, thuggish bouncer standing outside the door of our minds, attentively checking IDs and not allowing in any thought that doesn't meet the criteria of being true, noble, right, lovely, admirable, excellent, or praiseworthy. If a thought is inconsistent with God's Word, we will wrestle it to the ground and make it obedient to Christ. If a thought sets itself up against the knowledge of God, we will demolish it with divine power, because we will not be dominated by dark thoughts that are self-destructive and displeasing to God.

Who, Not What

Back to our thoughtology teacher, Paul.

Paul is in prison. Not for a crime but for speaking about Jesus. He may be executed. He writes to his friends in Philippi, "Rejoice in the Lord always" (Philippians 4:4). Then he sounds like your mama because he repeats himself, just in case you aren't listening. "I will say it again: Rejoice!"

It's a great verse for a coffee mug with a pretty cursive font: "Rejoice in the Lord always!" It's perfect for a refrigerator magnet. Put it on a greeting card? Of course! It makes you sound spiritual if you tell your friends, "Rejoice in the Lord always!"

Full disclosure: I hate it when people quote that verse to me. If I'm in the middle of a difficult situation, or I have a flat tire and it's 102 degrees out, or I just found out I need to have my tooth drilled, the last thing I want to hear is, "Craig, you just need to rejoice in the Lord always!"

One reason I hate it is because I have to wonder about the person who says it. *Do you rejoice in the Lord always? Really?*

You might wonder about Paul. He told people to rejoice in the Lord when he was in prison! But did *he* rejoice in the Lord when he was in prison?

He did.

The jail cell in Rome from which Paul wrote to his friends in Philippi was not the first time he was in prison. Paul was often imprisoned for preaching Jesus. We read about one of those times in Acts 16. Interestingly, this time Paul was in jail in Philippi.

Paul was with his buddy Silas. I assume Paul called him Si. If your buddy ain't got a nickname, he ain't a buddy.

Paul and Silas healed a woman, which upset some people and led to a riot.

"The crowd joined in the attack against Paul and Silas, and the magistrates ordered them to be stripped and beaten with rods. After they had been severely flogged, they were thrown into prison, and the jailer was commanded to guard them carefully. When he received these orders, he put them in the inner cell and fastened their feet in the stocks. About midnight Paul and Silas were praying and singing hymns to God, and the other prisoners were listening to them" (Acts 16:22–25).

While likely you've never been stripped and beaten with rods, you may have been stripped of your confidence, your faith, or your dignity and beaten with doubts, anxiety, or self-loathing. Perhaps you can relate to Paul and Silas a little.

Can you picture them? Thrown into prison, landing on the cold, hard ground with open wounds, maybe a broken nose, a couple of broken ribs. No doctor, nurse, bandages, or ibuprofen.

Have you been there? Perhaps you hit the ground when you found out someone you love had cancer or that your best friend was talking about you behind your back or that someone in your school died in a car accident. In those tragic moments, what do you do?

What did Paul and Silas do?

They praised God.

What was Paul doing in prison? Rejoicing always.

I wonder how it happened.

Maybe Paul leaned over and said, "Hey, Si."

"Yeah?"

"Si, we're not dead."

"That's true, Paul."

"So I was just thinking. If we're not dead, we're not done."

"That's right!"

"You know what else, Si? Our God is still on the throne. Jesus is risen, still at the right hand of the Father. He's praying for us!"

"Yasss!"

"Si, I think we need to give him a little praise. Why don't we worship him?"

I don't know if that's how it went down, but there are three things I do know.

First, they were praising God for the who, not the what.

They were bloody and bound up in prison. If you had asked them, "What are you praising God for?" I don't think there was any what they could point to. Nothing good was happening, but their God was still good. They weren't praising God for the what. They were praising him for the who. You can do that too.

Your circumstances may be bad, but your God is still good. He is near, his promises are still true, his love still unconditional, his grace still amazing, his timing still perfect. You may not like the what of what's going on, but you can still praise God for the who of who he is.

> Your circumstances may be bad, but your God is still good.

Second, they were praising God before things got better.

So often we hold off on praising God until he provides what we want. Think about that. Doesn't it sound like an entitled little snot-nosed kid? *I won't be grateful until I get exactly what I want.* You are better than that and, more important, God deserves better. Paul and Silas praised God before he answered their prayers or changed their circumstances. That's the kind of person I want to be.

Third, they were praising God and *then* he showed up.

Paul and Silas were worshiping God in the middle of the night and—boom!—God showed up. "Suddenly, there was a massive earthquake, and the prison was shaken to its foundations. All the doors immediately flew open, and the chains of every prisoner fell off!" (Acts 16:26 NLT).

They did not praise God because he showed up; God showed up because they praised him.

I wonder if it's possible that you've been praying for God to show up for you in some way, thinking you'll be grateful and praise him when he does, while God is waiting for you to be grateful and praise him, and won't show up until you do.

So let's rejoice in the Lord always. Let's worship him now, no matter our what, for who he is. Let's praise him and— spoiler alert—God will show up. He will shake your cell, chains will fall off, and doors will swing open.

Paul wrote, "Rejoice in the Lord always" to his friends in Philippi from his prison cell in Rome, because he had been in prison cells before, including in Philippi. He knew what happens when we praise God even before he provides. God shows up. God shows off.

It's time for us to fix our thoughts on God, to give him

praise for who he is, regardless of what he may or may not be doing.

When we praise him, he will show up.

When he shows up, it will change our thinking.

If we change our thoughts, we change our life.

Guess what? Even more will change. When we praise God, it also changes our perspective and our brain. And that's where we're going next.

your
God box

Through prayer and the power of God, we take every thought captive. Let me give you a visual way of thinking about this. (And I want you to actually do this.)

Get a box. It doesn't have to be fancy or big: a small Amazon box or a shoebox will work fine. Now write *God* on the box.

Every time you have a worry, burden, temptation, or runaway crazy thought, write it down on a slip of paper. You might write:

- ► I'm afraid I'm going to fail Chemistry.
- ► I want to get on my phone and go to websites or social media I know I shouldn't.
- ► I'm worried about how much my parents argue.
- ► I so badly want to be liked.
- ► I'm never going to change.
- ► I'm constantly angry with my mom.

Whatever worries come to mind, write them down and put them in your God box. When you do, pray, "God, I am trusting you with this. I know you are in control. I know you are bigger than this. This is not a thought I want to think, so I am giving this to you."

Once you pray and put the problem in the box, go on with your life.

From that point on, if you decide you want to worry about whatever it was, go to the God box, take it out, and tell God, "I don't trust you with this. I am going to take it back from you."

When you read that last sentence, you probably thought, *I could never say that to God,* but every time we worry or panic, that *is* what we're saying to God.

That is not how we want to live, and we don't need to live that way. Paul told us, "The Lord is near," so we need to practice God's presence so we'll be persistent in prayer. Peter told us we can cast all our cares on God because he cares for us. Our thoughts seek to betray us, but we know:

- ► If it's big enough to worry about, it's big enough to pray about.
- ► If it's on your mind, it's on God's heart.

"Let us then approach God's throne of grace with confidence, so that we may receive mercy and find grace to help us in our time of need" (Hebrews 4:16).

So get a box, write down your problems, pray about them, and put them inside. What if this simple exercise changes your prayer life and what God does in and around you?

the invisible *gorilla*

Five years before YouTube was even a thing, there was a viral video floating around the internet featuring a challenging attention test. The video showed three individuals in black shirts and three in white shirts bouncing a basketball to each other. Viewers were asked to silently keep track of how many times the people in white shirts passed the ball. At the end of the video, viewers weren't asked for the number of ball passes, but whether they saw someone in a gorilla costume walk across the screen, beat its arms against its chest, and walk away on the other side.[1]

Believe it or not, a little more than half of the viewers completely missed the gorilla. And even after being told it was there, most requested a second viewing in order to believe it was true.

The video and the experiment became an online sensation, turning researchers and psychologists Christopher Chabris and Daniel Simons into minor celebrities. Seriously, take a minute and look up "The Invisible Gorilla" and show the video to an unsuspecting friend—then see what happens.

The truth is we all suffer from inattentional blindness. We get so focused on watching the number of basketball passes that we miss the hairy gorilla beating its chest at us. We focus on the problems in front of us and miss that God is still in control, not beating his chest in frustration but opening his arms to hold us.

When we step back and shift our perspective to the big picture, learning to embrace God's presence through prayer and praise, something interesting happens.

The change of perspective leads us to praise God, and praising God changes our perspective.

Praising God is all about perspective.

The fourth tool I've learned that has powerfully impacted my thinking and my life is the Rejoice Principle: Revive your soul, reclaim your life. I stay mindful of God's presence; I praise him.

When I've had enough, I pray, putting my concerns in my God box.

I praise God—for the who, not the what—even when I don't want to.

And I sense my perspective changing.

Look at What's Right

Paul wanted to be in Rome, but not in a prison cell. He wanted to preach, not be a prisoner. Nothing was going the way he'd hoped.

From that jail, in chains, Paul wrote his letter to the Philippians. Remember part 3, when we saw how Paul reframed what he was going through? Instead of complaining that he couldn't preach to the government officials like he wanted, he praised God for the opportunity he'd been given to preach to the prison guards. He didn't feel thwarted; he was thrilled. He wrote, "Because of this I rejoice." Then he added, "Yes, and I will continue to rejoice, for I know that through your prayers and God's provision of the Spirit of Jesus Christ what has happened to me will turn out for my deliverance. I eagerly expect and hope that I will in no way be ashamed, but will have sufficient courage so that now as always Christ will be exalted in my body, whether by life or by death. For to me, to live is Christ and to die is gain" (Philippians 1:18–21).

While everything seemed negative, Paul chose to see the positive. Paul was looking at the big picture. He was seeing the image God wanted him to see that others couldn't. That's why, as he continued the letter, he wrote, "The Lord is near" (Philippians 4:5) and, "Do not be anxious about anything" (v. 6) and, "The peace of God, which transcends all understanding, will guard your hearts and your minds in Christ Jesus" (v. 7). It's why he could tell his readers, "Rejoice in the Lord always" (v. 4).

How could he praise God in jail? Perspective. It's not about prison but about perspective.

When we look through our circumstances with perspective, we know there is always reason to praise God.

Remember when I said the summer of 2019 was particularly tough for me as a pastor? After a particularly hard trip that happened while I was dealing with many stressful things going on at home, I returned and decided enough was enough—it was time to start seeing a counselor. At one appointment he asked me, "How bad is it?"

I told him, "I'm in trouble."

We went through a long series of questions. At the end my counselor said, "Well, I've got really good news for you. You're not in that much trouble."

I said, "No, you don't understand. I *am* in trouble."

He smiled. "No, you don't understand. You're not in that much trouble. I mean, I know trouble, and you're not in that much trouble. You have an issue that is very real, but when you look at everything else, you've got so much good in your life."

Because I was in panic mode, I looked at him suspiciously.

He said, "Physically, you're in really great shape. Your diet is almost flawless. You're not abusing any kind of substances. You're ridiculously in love with your wife. You have a great relationship with your kids. You're not missing family events. You've got incredible relationships around you, a lot of people who really care about you."

I nodded. Because he was right.

The counselor continued. "There are so many things that are right. The reason you're panicking is because you're just looking at what's wrong. Don't forget to also look at what's right."

He nailed it. I was counting the bounces, not seeing the gorilla. I was staring at my problems, having lost perspective on all the ways God had blessed my life. I left the counselor's office praising God.

I don't know what problems you're staring at right now. You might have a big one and a complicated one and an annoying one. I'm not minimizing your issues. I know they are real.

Teens today are facing problems the world has never seen before. Social media? Screens everywhere? All new.

Add in the fact that teenage brains are still learning how to navigate emotions, and you've got good reason for feeling stressed (even if you can't name exactly what it is you are feeling sometimes).

According to a study from Harvard and the University of Washington, teens tend to experience many emotions at the same time, but they have trouble telling them apart.* So if you are feeling sad and angry, it can be hard to name them both, which makes it harder to know how to deal with either emotion well.

Learning to identify and regulate your emotions is important, and a good way to practice this is through prayer—slowing down and mindfully asking God to help you understand the different things you are feeling.

*: Nook et. al., "The Nonlinear Development of Emotion Differentiation: Granular Emotional Experience Is Low in Adolescence," *https://journals.sagepub.com/doi/10.1177/0956797618773357.*

Let's just take a moment and recognize how hard things can be at your age.

Now let's take what might be an even harder step. We're going to take our focus off the challenge and problems.

Take a step back and look at the big picture. Do you have family? Friends? A church? Your health? A home? Some food in the fridge? Your faith?

Don't just look at what's wrong. Look at what's right. Maybe take a minute to write down all the good things. Literally count your blessings and thank God for them.

A change of perspective leads us to praise God.

And praising God changes our perspective.

> A change of perspective leads us to praise God. And praising God changes our perspective.

We often see this in the Psalms. The psalmist might begin by recounting what's wrong in his life: Enemies are attacking; he is feeling rejected by God; he's been falsely accused; he has spotty cell phone coverage. Then he commands himself to praise God anyway. Here are some examples:

- "Why, my soul, are you downcast? Why so disturbed within me? Put your hope in God, for I will yet praise him, my Savior and my God" (Psalm 42:5).
- "Bless the Lord, O my soul; and all that is within me, bless His holy name! Bless the Lord, O my soul, and forget not all His benefits" (Psalm 103:1–2 NKJV).
- "Praise the Lord! Praise the Lord, O my soul! While I live I will praise the Lord; I will sing praises to my God while I have my being" (Psalm 146:1–2 NKJV).

The psalmist is reading from the Bad Perspective Version but forces himself to praise God, and then—bam!—a changed perspective:

- "By day the Lord directs his love, at night his song is with me—a prayer to the God of my life" (Psalm 42:8).

▶ "The LORD has established his throne in heaven, and his kingdom rules over all. Praise the LORD, you his angels, you mighty ones who do his bidding, who obey his word. Praise the LORD, all his heavenly hosts, you his servants who do his will. Praise the LORD, all his works everywhere in his dominion. Praise the LORD, my soul" (Psalm 103:19–22).

That's what happened to me that day in my councilor's office. I was in the midst of panic, but I forced myself to praise, and praising God changed my perspective. I went from looking at my problems and seeing overwhelming obstacles to looking through my problems and seeing an omnipotent God who was right there with me.

Praising God changes our perspective.

And praising God changes our brains.

That's been verified too.

Praise, like prayer, affects the amygdala, diminishing the fight-or-flight mechanism.[2] Worshiping God has even been shown to decrease heart rate, blood pressure, blood glucose levels, and serum markers of inflammation.[3]

That's not all.

Remember Dr. Newberg, the brain scientist? He has proven that praising and worshiping God leads to quantifiable changes in brain volume and metabolism, especially in a part of the brain called the cingulate cortex. Turns out, an increase in the volume of the cingulate cortex results in increased capacity for compassionate thinking and feeling.[4] So, basically, the more the cingulate grows, the more empathetic you become.

Some studies suggest that the connectivity of the cingulate cortex in a teen's brain is related to your ability to regulate moods and better understand social dynamics. Teens whose cingulate cortex isn't as well connected are more likely to develop depression.*

*: Lichenstien et. al., "Adolescent Brain Development and Depression: A Case for the Importance of Connectivity of the Anterior Cingulate Cortex," https://pubmed.ncbi.nlm.nih.gov/27461914/.

That's what happened to me. After my appointment with my counselor, when I was stuck while writing my message, I made myself praise God. Praising him changed my perspective and gave me my message. Moments earlier I could not come up with a message, but then I felt overwhelmed by it.

I was writing a message about having a perspective of praise, even in the midst of anxiety. I realized I had not struggled much with anxiety or with not feeling like praising God. In the past, I could not have had deep empathy for the people I'd be speaking to, because I had never really felt it. But my miserable summer of angst had put me in that place, and I had to learn how to fix my thoughts and fight out of it. That's when it hit me. With a bad perspective, *I've had enough* and *I can't handle this* were all I could see, but through a perspective of praise, it became *I want you to know, brothers and sisters, that what has happened to me has served to advance the gospel.*

I felt more compassion for struggling people. I don't know if it was because I was pumping up my cingulate cortex, but I knew I couldn't wait to share this message with hurting people.

Praise changed my perspective.

I knew it would change theirs.

And I know it will change yours.

Don't Drop Your Guard

Are you ready for a complete non sequitur?

> A non sequitur is Latin for "it does not follow" and refers to a statement that is seemingly unconnected to a previous argument or statement. When your friends randomly change the subject in the middle of a conversation because they stopped listening a while back, that's a non sequitur.

I've got serious nunchuck skills. For real! I am legitimately good with nunchucks. I have taken classes in several martial arts: aikido, tae kwon do, and jiujitsu. Also, I have watched *The Karate Kid* (the original movie from the eighties, where Daniel from the more recent *Cobra Kai* was still a kid) probably thirty times, and I can do Mr. Miyagi's crane kick with the best of them.

My greatest training came from working with a childhood friend named Jody Nolan. Jody, who has black belts in several martial arts, became a professional stuntman and a sparring partner for Chuck Norris.

Back when we were in eleventh grade, we put on full pads and headgear. We were going at it. I felt like I was holding my own. I thought, *I really am pretty dang good.* That's when Jody asked, "Are you ready to go hard?" *Umm, I thought we were already going hard.* I knew I couldn't back down, so I looked at Jody and said, "Bring it." Jody brought it. The problem was that when I said, "Bring it," I think I was a little afraid, and I lowered my guard for a second. It went down like this:

> **Jody:** "Are you ready to go hard?"
> **Me:** "Bring it."
> **Jody:** Sends something—I think maybe a cinder block—crashing into my face. (I found out later Jody hit me with a spinning backfist that I never saw coming.)
> **Me:** Suddenly lying on my back, with little cartoon stars and birds spinning around my head.
> **Jody:** "You dropped your guard! I told you, never drop your guard. Whatever you do, don't drop your guard!"

As we near the end of our journey, I hope you walk away understanding that your thinking determines so much. Your life always moves in the direction of your strongest thoughts. What consumes your mind controls your life.

I also hope you remember that, unfortunately, your mind is under attack.

Just after encouraging us to humble ourselves and cast all our anxiety on God, Peter wrote, "Be alert and of sober mind. Your enemy the devil prowls around like a roaring lion looking for someone to devour" (1 Peter 5:8).

Peter said, "Be alert." Don't drop your guard! Why? You have an enemy, the devil, and he is looking for someone to devour. The devil is always coming after you, he is always swinging, and so you always have to keep your hands up.

How do we do that?

Remember what Paul wrote: "Do not be anxious about anything, but in every situation, by prayer and petition, with thanksgiving, present your requests to God. And the peace of God, which transcends all understanding, will guard your hearts and your minds in Christ Jesus" (Philippians 4:6–7).

Paul calls for us to make petitions (aka requests) and offer thanksgiving. Or we could say, prayer and praise. The promise is, if we do that, God will guard our minds. His peace will guard our minds.

Peace guards your heart and your mind.

Peace is preceded by prayer and praise.

In a fight, you need to keep both hands up to protect yourself. Think of prayer as one hand and praise as the other. We need to keep both hands raised.

When someone raises both hands, that can be to surrender or to celebrate a victory. When we raise both hands to God, it is both—surrendering to God and fully anticipating the victory that is already ours, because we know we are more than conquerors through him who loves us.

The devil's target is your mind. His weapon is his lies. He will never stop trying to deceive you. There are lies he's been telling you your entire life. Right now he's seeking out opportunities to tell you new lies. He is probably taking a swing at you as you read this, and he will again in the next few minutes, hours, days, and weeks.

What do we do?

We keep our guard up.

We go to God with prayer, and we go to God with praise.

Surrender *and* victory.

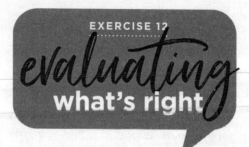

EXERCISE 12

evaluating
what's right

What circumstance or relationship in your life right now do you need to stop focusing on so you can instead look at the big picture to see what God is doing?

What circumstance or relationship in your life right now do you need to look at in a different way so you see what's right instead of seeing only what's wrong?

In what circumstance or relationship in your life right now have you dropped your guard and know you need to raise both hands to God, surrendering to him and fully anticipating the victory?

conclusion

Choosing to Win the War

Let's recap. Being a teenager has never been easy, but it's way more difficult today. You face battles, temptations, and stresses that didn't even exist when your parents were your age.

Social media is both entertaining, connecting, and a nightmare to navigate. Sexual temptation has always been a problem, but it's at a whole other level today. Bullying has been around forever, but it's much worse now that people can do it anonymously behind a screen. The rates of mental illness and suicide in teens are at a heartbreaking, all-time high. The world has always been complicated, but the tension and division that used to exist between different corners of a city are now often present in our own homes. The economy seems fragile. The future feels bleak. Our world is constantly at war. It's hard to know who to trust or where to turn. Our spiritual enemy seems to have more and more opportunities to trip you up, discourage you, depress you, and rob you of hope. (Don't stop reading. It gets better!)

That's why, like never before, you have to fight back. You have to choose to win the war in your mind. Although every day I feel like I have more than I can handle, I rely on God to renew my mind. His truth is my battle plan. I continue to create new trenches of truth to replace my old ruts so they will give me thought pathways leading to life and peace.

When I feel distracted by the things of this world, I will remind myself:

> Jesus is first in my life.
> I exist to serve and glorify him.

When I start to slide toward selfishness and take my blessings for granted, I will declare by faith:

> I will lay down my life and my desires
> sacrificially for others.

When I have a negative attitude about people and find myself criticizing others, I will write it, say it, and repeat it until I believe it:

> I love people and believe the best about others.

When I feel lazy and uncaring, I will remind myself of the truth:

> I am disciplined.
> Christ in me is stronger than
> the wrong desires in me.

When I'm feeling sorry for myself because my life is hard or the critics are loud, I will remember:

Pain is my friend.
I rejoice in suffering, because
Jesus suffered for me.

When I start to think that what I do doesn't matter, that I'm not making a difference, I will counter that lie with the truth:

If God could use Elijah, he can use me.
The world will be different and better
because I served Jesus today.

Where do *you* need Jesus today, right now?

Where are your thoughts falling short of his life-giving truth?

Are you stuck in a negative, hurtful, and poisonous rut?

What will you do?

You will use the four tools God has given us to fix our thoughts and win the war in our minds: (1) the Replacement Principle, (2) the Rewire Principle, (3) the Reframe Principle, and (4) the Rejoice Principle.

1. You will remove the lie and replace it with truth. We know we have an enemy who is seeking to destroy us. His weapon is the lie. Our weakness is believing lies, and if we believe a lie, it will affect our lives as if it were true.

The problem is that we don't realize the lies we believe are lies. If we knew, we wouldn't believe them. Hopefully, the lies you need to defeat are now clear to you.

2. You will create new trenches of truth. Our brains have neural pathways—mental ruts we created through repeatedly thinking the same thoughts—which trigger our automatic response to external stimuli. To stop a behavior, we need to remove the lie behind it and replace the neural pathway. We dig truth trenches.

How?

You renew your mind with God's truth. As you internalize Bible verses, they will become your new way of thinking and responding.

You will form personal declarations, writing them, thinking them, and confessing them until you believe them. These declarations of God's truth about you will become your new mental pathways to life and peace.

3. *You will reframe and preframe.* We cannot control what happens to us, but we can control how we perceive it. We all have cognitive biases that cause us to see things in ways that aren't real. But we have the power to do cognitive reframing, changing how we view the past and the future.

4. *You will change your perspective through prayer and praise.* It's easy to feel overwhelmed by everything that is happening, but when we've had enough, God is enough.

Not only is God enough; God is near. We stay mindful of his presence. When we do, it leads us to pray. Instead of worrying, we put all our fears in our God box, trusting his love and provision for us. Praying changes our brain, as does praising God. We praise him for the who of who he is, even if the what is not what we want. As we praise God, he shows up and gives us peace of mind.

Decide today that you will not think like the rest of the world. You will let God renew your mind.

Instead of becoming fixated on what you see, fix your

thoughts on Jesus. He made you. He will sustain you. He can carry you, strengthen you, and empower you to do what he's called you to do.

So don't drop your guard! Take captive every lie your enemy whispers in your ear. You know you are not someone who needs something other than God, because you know God is everything.

Remind yourself of the following truths daily, if not more often:

You are not controlled by fear.

You are not stuck.

You are not a slave to your habits.

You are not a prisoner to your addictions.

You are not a victim.

You are not failing.

You are not unlikable.

You are not unworthy of love.

You are not your past.

You are not what you did.

You are not what someone else did to you.

You are not who others say you are.

You are not who your unhealthy thoughts say you are.

You are not done.

You. Are. Who. God. Says. You. Are.

Because of Christ:

You are loved.

You are forgiven.

You are healed.

You are new.

You are redeemed.

You are free.

You are blessed.

You are strong and mighty.

You are chosen.

You are empowered.

You are a weapon of righteousness in a world of
darkness.

Let the truth about you trickle in, become a torrent, and
transform you.

Your God is with you. He will never leave you nor for-
sake you.

Your God is for you. He will fight for you. No weapon
formed against you will prosper. You are more than a conqueror through him.

Your God is enough for you. He is more than enough.

Nothing can separate you from God's love. Not death. Not
demons. Not the present nor the past. Nothing will ever separate you from the love of God that is in Christ Jesus our Lord.

Let God change your thinking.

He will change your life.

Appendix

Bible Verses for Winning the War

Use these passages in the exercises at the end of each chapter. Better yet, memorize them and think on them daily. Allow the words of God to renew your mind.

- ► Scripture quotations are listed in the order they appear in the book.
- ► When any Scripture reference is made in the book, the entire verse or passage is included here.
- ► Some verses are repeated in each of the four parts.
- ► Some verses are also available as downloadable graphics on my website so you can take them with you wherever you go. Those verses appear as bolded text here.

Introduction

Finally, brothers and sisters, whatever is true, whatever is noble, whatever is right, whatever is pure, whatever is lovely, whatever is admirable—if anything is excellent or praiseworthy—think about such things. Whatever you have learned or received or heard from me, or seen in me—put it into practice. And the God of peace will be with you.

—Philippians 4:8–9

As he thinks in his heart, so is he.

—Proverbs 23:7 NKJV

Part 1: The Replacement Principle
Remove the Lies, Replace with Truth

God has not given us a spirit of fear, but of power and of love and of a sound mind.

—2 Timothy 1:7 NKJV

We are not fighting against flesh-and-blood enemies, but against evil rulers and authorities of the unseen world, against mighty powers in this dark world, and against evil spirits in the heavenly places.

—Ephesians 6:12 NLT

"The thief comes only to steal and kill and destroy; I have come that they may have life, and have it to the full."

—John 10:10

Be alert and of sober mind. Your enemy the devil prowls around like a roaring lion looking for someone to devour.

—1 Peter 5:8

So I find this law at work: Although I want to do good, evil is right there with me. For in my inner being I delight in God's law; but I see another law at work in me, waging war against the law of my mind and making me a prisoner of the law of sin at work within me. What a wretched man I am! Who will rescue me from this body that is subject to death?

—Romans 7:21–24

I know what it is to be in need, and I know what it is to have plenty. I have learned the secret of being content in any and every situation, whether well fed or hungry, whether living in plenty or in want.

—Philippians 4:12

Though we live in the world, we do not wage war as the world does. The weapons we fight with are not the weapons of the world. On the contrary, they have divine power to demolish strongholds. We demolish arguments and every pretension that sets itself up against the knowledge of God, and we take captive every thought to make it obedient to Christ.

—2 Corinthians 10:3–5

I also pray that you will understand the incredible greatness of God's power for us who believe him. This is the same mighty power that raised Christ from the dead and seated him in the place of honor at God's right hand in the heavenly realms.

—Ephesians 1:19–20 NLT

Take the helmet of salvation and the sword of the Spirit, which is the word of God.

—Ephesians 6:17

Do not conform to the pattern of this world, but be transformed by the renewing of your mind. Then you will be able to test and approve what God's will is—his good, pleasing and perfect will.

—ROMANS 12:2

"Then you will know the truth, and the truth will set you free."

—JOHN 8:32

I can do all this through him who gives me strength.

—PHILIPPIANS 4:13

Rejoice in the Lord always. I will say it again: Rejoice!

—PHILIPPIANS 4:4

"Come to me, all you who are weary and burdened, and I will give you rest. Take my yoke upon you and learn from me, for I am gentle and humble in heart, and you will find rest for your souls. For my yoke is easy and my burden is light."

—MATTHEW 11:28-30

Cast all your anxiety on him because he cares for you.

—1 PETER 5:7

God is our refuge and strength,
an ever-present help in trouble.

—PSALM 46:1

What, then, shall we say in response to these things? If God is for us, who can be against us?

—ROMANS **8:31**

In all these things we are more than conquerors through him who loved us.

—ROMANS **8:37**

God demonstrates his own love for us in this: While we were still sinners, Christ died for us.

—ROMANS **5:8**

He who did not spare his own Son, but gave him up for us all—how will he not also, along with him, graciously give us all things?

—ROMANS **8:32**

You created my inmost being;
    you knit me together in my mother's womb.
I praise you because I am fearfully and
    wonderfully made;
    your works are wonderful,
    I know that full well.
My frame was not hidden from you
    when I was made in the secret
place,
    when I was woven together in the
depths of the earth.

> Your eyes saw my unformed body;
>> all the days ordained for me were
>> written in your book
>>> before one of them came to be.
>
> —Psalm 139:13-16

Part 2: The Rewire Principle
Rewire Your Brain, Renew Your Mind

> Do not conform to the pattern of this world, but be transformed by the renewing of your mind. Then you will be able to test and approve what God's will is—his good, pleasing and perfect will.
>
> —Romans 12:2

> I have hidden your word in my heart
>> that I might not sin against you.
>
> —Psalm 119:11

> I know what it is to be in need, and I know what it is to have plenty. I have learned the secret of being content in any and every situation, whether well fed or hungry, whether living in plenty or in want.
>
> —Philippians 4:12

> God is able to bless you abundantly, so that in all things at all times, having all that you need, you will abound in every good work.
>
> —2 Corinthians 9:8

God will meet all your needs according to the riches of his glory in Christ Jesus.

—Philippians 4:19

Jesus replied, "I am the bread of life. Whoever comes to me will never be hungry again. Whoever believes in me will never be thirsty."

—John 6:35 NLT

What, then, shall we say in response to these things? If God is for us, who can be against us? He who did not spare his own Son, but gave him up for us all—how will he not also, along with him, graciously give us all things? Who will bring any charge against those whom God has chosen? It is God who justifies. Who then is the one who condemns? No one. Christ Jesus who died—more than that, who was raised to life—is at the right hand of God and is also interceding for us. Who shall separate us from the love of Christ? Shall trouble or hardship or persecution or famine or nakedness or danger or sword? As it is written:

"For your sake we face death all day long;
we are considered as sheep to be slaughtered."

No, in all these things we are more than conquerors through him who loved us. For I am convinced that neither death nor life, neither angels nor demons, neither the present nor the future, nor any powers, neither height nor depth, nor anything else in all creation, will be able to separate us from the love of God that is in Christ Jesus our Lord.

—Romans 8:31-39

Those who are dominated by the sinful nature think about sinful things, but those who are controlled by the Holy Spirit think about things that please the Spirit. So letting your sinful nature control your mind leads to death. But letting the Spirit control your mind leads to life and peace.

—ROMANS 8:5–6 NLT

"Keep this Book of the Law always on your lips; meditate on it day and night, so that you may be careful to do everything written in it. Then you will be prosperous and successful."

—JOSHUA 1:8

Within your temple, O God,
    we meditate on your unfailing love.

—PSALM 48:9

I will consider all your works
    and meditate on all your mighty deeds.

—PSALM 77:12

Cause me to understand the way of your precepts,
    that I may meditate on your
wonderful deeds.

—PSALM 119:27

I remember the days of long ago;
    I meditate on all your works
    and consider what your hands have done.

—PSALM 143:5

They speak of the glorious splendor of your
> majesty—
>> and I will meditate on your
>> wonderful works.
>>>> —Psalm 145:5

Part 3: The Reframe Principle
Reframe Your Mind, Restore Your Perspective

Trust in the Lord with all your heart,
> and do not lean on your own
> understanding.
In all your ways acknowledge him,
> and he will make straight your
> paths.
>>>> —Proverbs 3:5–6 ESV

"My thoughts are not your thoughts,
> neither are your ways my ways,"
> declares the Lord.
"As the heavens are higher than the earth,
> so are my ways higher than your ways
> and my thoughts than your
> thoughts."
>>>> —Isaiah 55:8–9

This is the day that the Lord has made;
> let us rejoice and be glad in it.
>>>> —Psalm 118:24 ESV

Part 4: The Rejoice Principle
Revive Your Soul, Reclaim Your Life

Praise the LORD.
Give thanks to the LORD, for he is good;
　　his love endures forever.

—PSALM 106:1

Rejoice in the Lord always. I will say it again: Rejoice! Let your gentleness be evident to all. The Lord is near. Do not be anxious about anything, but in every situation, by prayer and petition, with thanksgiving, present your requests to God. And the peace of God, which transcends all understanding, will guard your hearts and your minds in Christ Jesus.

—PHILIPPIANS 4:4-7

The LORD is righteous in all his ways
　　and faithful in all he does.
The LORD is near to all who call on him,
　　to all who call on him in truth.
He fulfills the desires of those who fear him;
　　he hears their cry and saves them.

—PSALM 145:17-19

Humble yourselves, therefore, under God's mighty hand, that he may lift you up in due time. Cast all your anxiety on him because he cares for you.

—1 PETER 5:6-7

Do not conform to the pattern of this world, but be transformed by the renewing of your mind. Then you will be able to test and approve what God's will is—his good, pleasing and perfect will.

—ROMANS 12:2

Those who are dominated by the sinful nature think about sinful things, but those who are controlled by the Holy Spirit think about things that please the Spirit. So letting your sinful nature control your mind leads to death. But letting the Spirit control your mind leads to life and peace.

—ROMANS 8:5-6 NLT

Let us then approach God's throne of grace with confidence, so that we may receive mercy and find grace to help us in our time of need.

—HEBREWS 4:16

I will continue to rejoice, for I know that through your prayers and God's provision of the Spirit of Jesus Christ what has happened to me will turn out for my deliverance. I eagerly expect and hope that I will in no way be ashamed, but will have sufficient courage so that now as always Christ will be exalted in my body, whether by life or by death. For to me, to live is Christ and to die is gain.

—PHILIPPIANS 1:18-21

Why, my soul, are you downcast?
Why so disturbed within me?
Put your hope in God,
for I will yet praise him,
my Savior and my God.

—Psalm 42:5

Bless the Lord, O my soul;
And all that is within me,
Bless His holy name!
Bless the Lord, O my soul,
And forget not all His benefits.

—Psalm 103:1–2 NKJV

By day the Lord directs his love,
at night his song is with me—
a prayer to the God of my life.

—Psalm 42:8

Praise the Lord, all his heavenly hosts,
you his servants who do his will.
Praise the Lord, all his works
everywhere in his dominion.
Praise the Lord, my soul.

—Psalm 103:21–22

Be alert and of sober mind. Your enemy the devil prowls around like a roaring lion looking for someone to devour.

—1 Peter 5:8

Acknowledgments

I'd like to express my deepest gratitude to all my friends who helped make this book possible.

Amy Groeschel, you are my best friend forever. Thank you for being "overboard for God" with me for three decades and counting.

Vince Antonucci, you are the best of the best of the best. I sincerely thank God for your friendship all these years. Your passion, creativity, and love for this message is evident on every single page. Your gifts are rare and special. Thank you for sharing them with me to expand the reach of our ministry. I'm profoundly thankful for you.

To Josh Mosey, you are a genius. Thank you for pouring your heart into each page to help this book connect deeply with a generation I love and believe in with all my heart. Your work will touch so many lives.

Megan Dobson, thank you for asking the hard questions, raising important issues, and pushing hard to make this message stronger. Your passion for this project shows.

To you, the reader, thank you for taking the journey with me. I know you are facing challenges that are so different and infinitely more complicated than those who are older than you. Thankfully, you have access to a power greater than all our temptations, mental health issues, or pressure. So let's do this together. Press into Jesus. Grab those thoughts that are contrary to his truth. Replace the lies you believe with God's unchanging truth. Change your thinking. And let God change your life.

notes

Introduction : What Makes the Teenage Brain Unique?
1. "What Is CBT Psychology, and What Are Its Benefits?" *betterhelp.com* (updated August 26, 2022), *www.betterhelp.com /advice/psychologists/what-is-cbt-psychology-and-what-are-its -benefits.*

Chapter 3: Old Lies, New Truth
1. Cheryl D. Fryar, MSPH, Margaret D. Carroll, MSPH, and Joseph Afful, MS, "Prevalence of Overweight, Obesity, and Severe Obesity Among Children and Adolescents Aged 2–19 Years: United States, 1963–1965 Through 2017–2018," NCHS Health E-Stats, 2020, accessed 8/24/2022, *https://www.cdc.gov /nchs/data/hestat/obesity-child-17-18/obesity child.htm.*
2. "Body Positivity Toolkit for Parents," Maxine Platzer Lynn Center at the University of Virginia, *https://womenscenter.virginia.edu /sites/womenscenter/files/2022-10Body%20Positive%20Toolkit%20 letter%20sized%20sept%202022.pdf.*
3. "Eating Disorders," NIH/National Institute of Mental Health, accessed 8/24/2022, *https://www.nimh.nih.gov/health/statistics /eating-disorders#part_2569.*
4. "Generation M²: Media in the Lives of 8- to 18-Year-Olds," Kaiser Family Foundation, 2010 study, accessed online 8/24/2022, *https://www.kff.org/wp-content/uploads/2013/01/8010.pdf.*
5. "Underage Drinking," NIH/National Institute on Alcohol Abuse and Alcoholism, accessed 8/24/2022, *https://www.niaaa.nih.gov /publications/brochures-and-fact-sheets/underage-drinking.*
6. "Marijuana Use and Teens," cdc.gov, accessed 8/24/2022, *https:// www.cdc.gov/marijuana/factsheets/pdf/MarijuanaFactSheets-Teens -508compliant.pdf.*
7. "Ian's Story," Courage to Speak Foundation, accessed 8/24/2022, *https://couragetospeak.org/courage-to-speak-stories-ians-story/.*

Chapter 4: Crossed Wires and Circular Ruts

1. "Distribution of Licensed Drivers—by Sex and Percentage in Each Age Group and Relation to Population," Federal Highway Association studies from 1996 and 2020; 1996: *https://www.fhwa.dot.gov/policyinformation/statistics/1996/pdf/dl20.pdf*; 2020: *https://www.fhwa.dot.gov/policyinformation/statistics/2020/dl20.cfm*.
2. "Buick Century Turbo Coupe," *Car and Driver*, June 1979, quoted page archived online at *https://i0.wp.com/www.curbsideclassic.com/wp-content/uploads/2017/11/CD0679-CenturyTurbo-p2.jpeg*.
3. "Bias (n.)," Online Etymology Dictionary, *https://www.etymonline.com/word/bias*.

Chapter 5: Creating a Trench of Truth

1. Jena E. Pincott, "Wicked Thoughts," *Psychology Today* (September 1, 2015; last updated June 10, 2016), *www.psychologytoday.com/us/articles/201509/wicked-thoughts*.

Chapter 6: Rumination and Renewal

1. Cow facts adapted from "27 Amazing Facts about Cows That Will Impress Your Friends," posted by Matt and Jessica of Clover Meadows Beef, July 14, 2022, *https://www.clovermeadowsbeef.com/amazing-facts-about-cows/*.
2. Emily Dreyfuss, "Want to Make a Lie Seem True? Say It Again. And Again. And Again," *Wired.com* (February 11, 2017), *www.wired.com/2017/02/dont-believe-lies-just-people-repeat*.

Chapter 7: Lenses and Filters

1. A. Wilke and R. Mata, "Cognitive Bias," in *Encyclopedia of Human Behavior*, 2nd ed., ed. V. S. Ramachandran (Burlington, MA: Academic Press, 2012), *www.sciencedirect.com/topics/neuroscience/cognitive-bias*.
2. Wei-chin Hwang, "Practicing Mental Strengthening," in *Culturally Adapting Psychotherapy for Asian Heritage Populations* (Burlington, MA: Academic Press, 2016), *www.sciencedirect.com/topics/psychology/cognitive-reframing*.

Chapter 9: Collateral Goodness

1. From Shemot Rabbah 24:1, taken from *https://rabbi360.com /2020/02/06/through-the-mud-to-the-promised-land/*.

Chapter 10: Problems, Panic, and Presence

1. Will Dunham, "Hormone Paradox May Help Explain Teen Moodiness," Reuters, March 12, 2007, *https://www.reuters.com /article/us-puberty-hormone-idUSN0940699220070312*.
2. Brian E. Robertson, PhD, "The 90-Second Rule that Builds Self-Control," *Psychologytoday.com*, posted April 26, 2020, accessed 8/31/2022, *https://www.psychologytoday.com/us/blog /the-right-mindset/202004/the-90-second-rule-builds-self-control*.
3. Sandy Cohen, "Suicide Rate Highest Among Teens and Young Adults," UCLA Health, March 15, 2022, *https://connect .uclahealth.org/2022/03/15/suicide-rate-highest-among-teens -and-young-adults/*.

Chapter 11: The Perspective of Praise

1. See *www.drleaf.com/pages/about-dr-leaf*, accessed 8/31/2022.
2. Quoted in Megan Kelly, "How Prayer Changes the Brain and Body," *Renewing All Things* (June 9, 2015), *https:// renewingallthings.com/how-prayer-changes-the-brain-and-body*.
3. Michael Liedke, "Neurophysiological Benefits of Worship," *Journal of Biblical Foundations of Faith and Learning* 3, no. 1 (2018): 5, *https://knowledge.e.southern.edu/cgi/viewcontent .cgi?article=1063&context=jbffl*.

Chapter 12: The Invisible Gorilla

1. "Bet You Didn't Notice the 'Invisible Gorilla,'" NPR *Talk of the Nation*, May 19, 2010, accessed online at *https://www.npr.org /2010/05/19/126977945/bet-you-didnt-notice-the-invisible-gorilla*. Video can be viewed at *http://www.theinvisiblegorilla.com/gorilla _experiment.html*.
2. Peter A. Boelens et al., "A Randomized Trial of the Effect of Prayer on Depression and Anxiety," *International Journal of*

Psychiatry in Medicine 39, no. 4 (January 2009): 377–92, *www.researchgate.net/publication/43146858_A_Randomized _Trial_of_the_Effect_of_Prayer_on_Depression_and_Anxiety.* Cited in Liedke, "Neurophysiological Benefits of Worship," 6.

3. James W. Anderson and Paige A. Nunnelley, "Private Prayer Associations with Depression, Anxiety and Other Health Conditions: An Analytical Review of Clinical Studies," *Postgraduate Medicine* 128, no. 7 (July 2016): 635–41, *www.researchgate.net/publication/305630281_Private_praye _associations_with_depression_anxiety_and_other_health _conditions_an_analytical_review_of_clinical_studies.* Cited in Liedke, "Neurophysiological Benefits of Worship," 6.

4. Karen L. Kuchan, "Prayer as Therapeutic Process toward Aliveness within a Spiritual Direction Relationship," *Journal of Religion and Health* 47, no. 2 (July 2008): 263–75, *www.researchgate.net/publication/23686585_Prayer_as _Therapeutic_Process_Toward_Aliveness_Within_a_Spiritual _Direction_Relationship.* Cited in Liedke, "Neurophysiological Benefits of Worship," 6.

Winning the War in Your Mind

Craig Groeschel

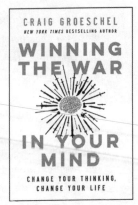

Are your thoughts out of control—just like your life? Do you long to break free from the spiral of destructive thinking? Let God's truth become your battle plan to win the war in your mind!

Pastor and *New York Times* bestselling author Craig Groeschel understands deeply this daily battle against self-doubt and negative thinking, and in this powerful book he reveals the strategies he's discovered to change your mind and your life for the long-term.

Drawing upon Scripture and the latest findings of brain science, Groeschel lays out practical strategies that will free you from the grip of harmful, destructive thinking and enable you to live the life of joy and peace God intends you to live. *Winning the War in Your Mind* will help you:

- Learn how your brain works and see how to rewire it
- Identify the lies your enemy wants you to believe
- Recognize and short-circuit your mental triggers for destructive thinking
- See how prayer and praise will transform your mind
- Develop practices that allow God's thoughts to become your thoughts

God has something better for your life than your old ways of thinking. It's time to change your mind so God can change your life.

Available wherever books are sold!